Cover Girl

Cover Girl

Brittani Williams

www.urbanbooks.net

Urban Books, LLC
78 East Industry Court
Deer Park, NY 11729

ISBN 13: 978-1-60162-502-1
ISBN 10: 1-60162-502-2

First Printing November 2011
Printed in the United States of America

10 9 8 7 6 5 4 3 2 1

Distributed by Kensington Publishing Corp.
Submit Wholesale Orders to:
Kensington Publishing Corp.
C/O Penguin Group (USA) Inc.
Attention: Order Processing
405 Murray Hill Parkway
East Rutherford, NJ 07073-2316
Phone: 1-800-526-0275
Fax: 1-800-227-9604

Cover Girl

A Novel

By

Brittani Williams

Author of *Daddy's Little Girl, Black Diamond, Sugar Walls,* and *Black Diamond 2: Nicety*

Dedication

Cover Girl is dedicated to Faith Johnson who was my inspiration for this novel. She is a true survivor!

Acknowledgments

First I'd like to thank God for pulling me through once again. This has been an amazing journey for me and I am truly blessed and humbled.

My son, Kristion, I love you and I will continue to strive harder each day for you. It is because of you that I keep going on, on those days when I'm dead tired!

To my Mom and Dad, thanks for continuing to be the supportive parents that you are. I really appreciate you all believing in me. I love you.

To Damon thanks for being you! We will always remain friends regardless of what happens between us. You are very special to me and I will always love you.

Mary, my bestfriend, I love you honey! I am glad that you are back in Philly and I hope that you don't leave any time soon!

To all of my friends Jennifer, Nikki, Bebe, and Kai you girls are the best!

Tameka Nelson and Rosie Bonds . . . Thanks for coming into my life and becoming the great friends that you both are.

To Najla, I love you and I thank you for all of your help and support!

Alicia and Frances, I love you both and thanks for being there to talk to when I needed it.

Sharmina T. Ellis, thanks for being the best publicist in the world! You are truly a godsend and I look forward to working with you for many years to come.

Acknowledgments

To Davida Baldwin, thanks for the dope pics and the awesome cover! You have always been pretty patient with my many requests and I appreciate that.

To Vanessa Lynn and Angela Barrow Dunlap, thanks for all of your support, knowledge, and inspiration. You two are amazing and I can only hope to be as successful as you one day.

To Sean Hughes, thanks for believing in my vision you have truly been a blessing.

Shout out to Anna J., Dashawn Taylor, K'wan, T. Styles, Anya Nicole, and all of the other authors out there doing their thing! We have to stay focused and keep pushing for black literature.

Thanks to Carl Weber and Urban Books for your confidence in me. I am looking forward to putting these books out and getting busy!

To Ramona's touch of essence salon, thanks for the amazing job with my stage play!

To all of my fans you all have been the absolute best! Thank you for your continued support and I promise I won't be leaving the game any time soon. Thanks to the over 700 people who came out to see Black Diamond the stage play! It was a huge success and I look forward to doing more plays in the very near future.

To those that I have forgotten, please charge it to my mind and not my heart!

I love you all!

Visit my website www.BrittaniWilliams.com to stay up to date!

Prologue

Winter Storm

Thanksgiving Day had never been remarkable prior to this one. Turkey, baked macaroni and cheese, candied yams, collard greens and cornbread stuffing are all one could normally think of when speaking of the festivities surrounding this day of giving thanks for all of one's blessings, but on this particular day, November 25, 2007, blessings were the last thing on Brooklyn's mind. In fact, she couldn't fathom one thing to be thankful for. Not even her life felt like a blessing. Hell, for her, the energy it took just to stay alive at this point wasn't worth the misery and embarrassment.

"Hey, Brooklyn, you got a late start today, I see," one of her fellow addicts called out as she headed toward the shooting gallery upstairs.

"Yeah. Had a lot of shit on my mind, that's all. But you know me. Nothing can hold me down." She forced a laugh, though she felt like the walls were caving in on her, that she would have to fight extremely hard to pull through.

Brooklyn stood peering aimlessly out of the window as the setting sun gently displayed patches of shade onto one side of the street. A mixture of ice and snow continued to fall from the sky, turning the streets into what resembled an ice skating rink. The crackhouse, which she frequented daily to get high, was clouded with smoke, and reeked of urine and feces from the various hidden crevices where the fiends had released themselves. She felt like she wanted to puke.

She rested the right side of her thin frame up against the old wooden windowsill, her feet relaxed on the badly frayed rippled linoleum flooring. Her face full of dismay, she wasn't thinking about getting high or having jumped over the missing steps at the entrance of the building, all the while praying not to land on her ass in the basement. Nor the hole in the wall of the adjacent house that she had to climb through to get into the room where she now stood. Nor the numerous mice crawling, weaving in and out of holes in the walls, or the drug dealers in the other room selling their product to the fiends.

For the moment, all Brooklyn could think about was being just three short blocks away from her mother's home and too embarrassed to go spend the holidays with her family. She had just been diagnosed with cervical cancer and hadn't yet been able to reveal this to them. After years of unprotected sex and several untreated sexually transmitted diseases, her reckless behavior had finally run up and kicked her in the ass.

Brooklyn couldn't have cared less that she was losing her hair, or breaking out with bumps all over her face, and rashes that covered fifty percent of her body, all the result of the multiple illegal drugs she shot into her system daily. Though she'd always been the bad seed of the family, having an illness like cancer would make them feel sorry for her, and she wasn't interested in sympathy, not wanting to appear weak.

Fiends filled each room all at different levels of their high. The house was cold, only having heat in one room, which was obtained by running extension cords from the house next door. From the outside, one would assume the house was empty. With a huge orange sticker on the front of it labeling it unsafe, and the front door and most of the windows boarded up, normal people, like those not under the influence of drugs, wouldn't even be caught dead on that side of the street.

Brooklyn's mind was all over the place. She thought about her modeling career, about how'd she'd allowed herself to lose everything she'd worked for, her many failed attempts at relationships, and of course her children, one of whom she hadn't seen since he was six months old. But regardless of which path her mind would follow, the road would always end at the same destination, Dover Street.

Dover Street was in the northern part of Philadelphia. All of the houses, which were pretty small, had once been full of life and excitement but were mostly empty now. No matter how hard she tried, she could never stay away from the block very long.

This morning she woke up, quickly got dressed, and hurried to the house to try and beat the rush. Today felt different, even down to the dogs barking on the corner and the wind that blew ice in her face as she struggled to see through it. She'd arrived a few minutes later than normal and found all of her buddies already floating on cloud nine. They'd created a "snowball," a mixture of heroin and cocaine which they would place inside of a glass pipe, put fire to, and smoke. Instead of joining in, she was drawn to the window where her feet had been planted for the past twenty minutes.

Joey, one of the dealers who ran the house, yelled from the doorway, "Yo, Brooklyn, are you going to cop or what? You know you can't stay here if you're not. This ain't no goddamn recreation center!"

The vibration of Joey's voice startled everyone in the room, especially JC, who'd just wrapped his brown leather belt around his upper arm, preparing to shoot his heated concoction into his bulging vein.

Brooklyn snapped out of her daydream. She turned to face him before taking a step away from the window. "Yeah, Joey. I'm sorry. I have some shit on my mind."

Joey's look of disgust changed to anger. "Well, you know the rules," he yelled. "So what's on your mind is some personal shit that you can take outside, if you ain't getting high." He motioned his hands toward the door.

"I said I'm gonna cop, Joey. Damn! I come here every day, and I always cop, so you don't have to try to play me. Just give me a minute, OK." Brooklyn hated that her moment of deep thought had been ruined.

"Yeah, a minute is all you're gonna get too!" he roared. "I'll be back in here to check, and you better either have some money in your hand, or the handle of the front door on your way out!" He turned around and walked through the halls, checking in on some of the other patrons of the house, the thumping noises from his large feet fading as he moved away from the room.

Brooklyn wanted to get high. In fact, her body was yearning for drugs, but her troubles had a grip on her thoughts and she was having trouble releasing them as she resumed her position, staring out into the ice storm. So far, the time had gone by without incident, but it was still early. There was rarely a dull moment in the house, also known as "The Tower," where mayhem could erupt at the drop of a dime. Either someone was getting thrown out for nonpayment or being carried out when they overdosed.

She quickly turned around when she heard footsteps nearing the door. Joey was back as promised. She dug into the pocket of her jeans and pulled out the folded twenty-dollar bill she had inside. The same twenty dollars she'd earned from giving oral sex to one of the sloppiest men she'd ever seen was a few moments away from being gone with the wind. One thing about Brooklyn, she always managed to get enough money to support her habit, even if it meant stealing from her own relatives and friends.

Joey motioned with his hands for her to follow him, and she walked behind him toward the room with the drug supplies. She stopped just outside of the door, as she normally did, and waited patiently to be served like a child in the lunch line.

Joey knocked on the door, which was bolted shut, and called out the items he needed. A bodyguard stood next to Joey, his hands in his pocket, firmly gripping his handgun, in case one of the crackheads got out of hand and had to be taken care of. Through a makeshift mail slot in the center of the brown wooden door, a bag filled with vials of crack cocaine inside of a sandwich bag was passed into his hand. He turned around, took the money from Brooklyn's extended hand, and replaced it with the bag of drugs.

She then walked away, returning to the room where she was prior to walking down the long hallway with him. She grabbed a seat off to the far right side of the room and sat down, trying to get comfortable.

Brooklyn took a quick surveillance and noticed Stacey shooting a mixture that she'd just heated into her veins. Stacey's eyes rolled into the back of her head within seconds as her body relaxed and her arm rested at her side. Brooklyn stared at her, anxious to get the same feeling, but her mind was still fixated on the test results her doctor had read to her earlier in the week.

Over and over in her head, she repeated, *Cancer? How the hell did I get cancer? Out of all the ailments I could get, why cancer?*

After a few more minutes of sulking in her misery, she opened up the bag of drugs and began the steps that would land her in the relaxing state she needed to be. Ten minutes later she was in a fantasy world, still sitting in the chair, her head resting on the back of it. The room was quiet, and the smell in the air made it that much more tranquil.

She had almost fallen asleep when a loud thump stunned her. Stacey had fallen down on the floor and began convulsing. Everyone in the room was now focusing their attention on her as her body continued to jerk and foam ran out of her mouth and down the sides of her face. "Somebody call nine-one-one!" Brooklyn yelled as she got down on her knees next to her.

"Nobody move! Mack, carry her ass out and put her in the lot down the street!" Joey yelled, his tone cold and steady as ice.

Brooklyn looked at him, filled with anger. She knew from past experiences that he was heartless. Any other time she'd get into a corner and watch the drama unfold, but Stacey was one of her friends, and she wasn't ready to lose her just yet.

"Call nine-one-one now," she yelled. "Don't put her out in the street like a piece of garbage." She tried to push Mack's hands away from Stacey's body.

"Back off, Brooklyn, before I put your ass out there with her. Mack, hurry up before this bitch dies on the floor," Joey yelled back. He hated when fiends got sick in the house. He knew it was always a possibility and was seriously thinking about moving his business to another part of the neighborhood separate from where they got high.

"She'll die out there, Joey. Please don't put her out there." Brooklyn's eyes began to well up with tears. She was practically in a tug-of-war with Mack, trying to keep him from putting Stacey out.

"I don't give a fuck about that!" Joey yelled. "She's not going to die up in here and have the cops come raid my shit. Hell, naw! Mack, put that bitch out now!" He pushed Brooklyn out of the way.

Mack picked Stacey's limp body up from the floor and put her over his shoulder. Brooklyn thought for sure she was already gone. She stared back at Joey. As the two watched each other, Brooklyn briefly reminisced on the good times they'd spent together when they dated during her modeling days. The man she once cared for stared right through her, almost as if she had translucent skin. Joey gave her a look of seriousness that ended all hope she had of changing his mind. Either way, she didn't plan on leaving Stacey out there for dead alone in the storm.

Brooklyn ran out behind Mack, who was looking left and right as he hurried down the street. Tears streamed down her face as she watched the life drain out of her friend's body. Stacey looked like a rag doll as she hung over Mack's shoulder.

Mack walked into the lot and dropped Stacey down on the ground. She hit the ice-covered lot like a ton of bricks. He walked out of the lot and headed toward the house without even looking back.

Brooklyn called Mack's name as he neared the sidewalk, almost gone from her eyesight.

"What?" Mack shouted, not even turning around to face her.

"Please call nine-one-one. Please, I'm begging you," Brooklyn cried, trying to save her dying friend.

As Mack walked away, Brooklyn let out a sigh of helplessness. She took off her coat, wrapped it around Stacey's cold body, and picked her head up from the ground. Stacey's eyes were closed, and her body was quickly dropping in temperature. She was still breathing, but that didn't mean she'd make it.

Brooklyn rubbed her hand across her forehead, looking around, hoping someone would arrive to help. She kept praying that Stacey would be OK, though her mind was telling her otherwise. Her knees were becoming stiff, but she refused to move. Stacey would have done the same for her. At least she forced herself to believe that.

"Help me, please. Somebody help me!" Brooklyn screamed as she grabbed hold of Stacey's shoulders and shook her as hard as she could. "Don't die on me, Stacey, please." Stacey's lips were slowly turning blue, and as loud as Brooklyn screamed her name, she got no response. She could feel the life draining out of Stacey's body with each passing second.

How had things come to this? How had things gone so wrong? As Stacey's almost lifeless body lay in front of Brooklyn, so many thoughts ran through her mind, including the decisions that landed her where she was that day. After all, Stacey was the one who got her hooked in the first place. Was this the lesson she needed to finally quit?

Brooklyn could remember as clear as day her first hit over eighteen years ago. She could also remember the special times they'd had, regardless of how screwed up things would get. She missed her friend already, just facing the idea of losing her. She wondered what she'd do without her right hand. In her eyes, she had nothing to live for with Stacey gone. Brooklyn's family despised her, and she'd done her children so wrong, they wouldn't even speak to her, even if she entered a room in which they were seated.

Brooklyn looked down at Stacey's face and saw her own. She saw her beautiful high cheekbones, long eyelashes, almond-shaped eyes, caramel complexion, and her perfectly full lips. Actually, Brooklyn saw the way she *used* to look, instead of her thin facial structure and the red blotches that covered her sunken cheeks. She didn't see her tired eyes and the dark circles underneath them. Neither did she see her dry, cracked lips, nor her hair that was as coarse as a Brillo pad.

The beautiful woman that she used to be had disappeared. Even if she quit shooting and inhaling all of the poison she did daily, that woman could never return. So what could she do? At that moment she wished she was the one dying instead of Stacey, but then her life would most likely have been spared. Death was something she'd stared in the eye on many occasions, but for some reason, God had always left her here to see another day.

What is He trying to tell me? Is there something else that I'm supposed to be doing?

Brooklyn got up from the ground. She thought she could run and get help for Stacey if she could just pull her out of the lot and into one of the houses. She grabbed her by the arms and tried dragging her, but weighing no more than 110 pounds soaking wet, she couldn't move her more than a few inches. She got back in position beside her, deciding she'd wait there with her until someone arrived to aid them. Her own body was stiffening to the point where she could no longer feel her limbs, or even her fingers that rested on Stacey's forehead. Was she finally going to get her wish? At least that's what she hoped.

In the distance Brooklyn could hear sirens, but she couldn't move to meet them at the street. If anyone was looking for them, it would be almost impossible for the duo to be found, as the sun was going down and the alley was darkening. Her voice wasn't as loud as it was previously. In fact, she could barely catch her breath as she felt herself getting weaker by the second. Maybe this was it. Maybe this was the way her life was supposed to end—in a dark alley, like a piece of trash.

Suddenly the sirens became inaudible, and her body fell to the ground next to Stacey's. Her head rested on Stacey's arm. Her eyes slowly closed, her body mirroring the unresponsive figure next to her.

Chapter One

Career Day
1985

The school hallways were filled with commotion. It was career day, and the students of Roberts Vaux Middle School took advantage of their free day. No one ever paid attention during career day, at least not the popular kids anyway. Brooklyn and her group of friends, which included Rene, Stacey, and Wanda, all picked the same career interests to guarantee they'd be together all day. They were the girls everyone loved to hate and the epitome of perfection in the eyes of most of their peers—all beautiful, smart, and talented in their own way.

Brooklyn, the youngest but the leader of the pack, was hands down the most stunning. She resembled one of those high-fashion models you'd see on TV, and her wardrobe only added to her look. She had flawless skin and the fair complexion of a "butter-pecan Rican" with glistening bronze highlights. Her teeth were straight without the help of braces or retainers and white enough to be featured in a Colgate commercial. Her hair hung below her shoulders, but she would often pull it back into a loose ponytail or wear it straight with little bends at the end. Her large almond-shaped eyes with light brown hue were just as striking. At fifteen, she was tall for her age, standing at almost five foot nine. Her body was fully developed with just the right amount of curves to wrap around her thin frame.Brooklyn's mother, who worked at Girard College during the day but bar-hopped at night, was close friends with the neighborhood boosters, so Brooklyn always donned the latest name-brand gear and accessories.

Rene was the loudmouth of the bunch. She wasn't as pretty as Brooklyn, but her personality made her stand out and always made her the center of attention. She was about five foot five, with a stocky frame, and what you'd call solid. She was always the first one to throw a punch in a fight and seldom the loser in any battle. But, for Rene, education was a must, and oftentimes when the rest of the girls would be goofing off, she'd have her head buried in the books. Her group of friends frequently leaned on her for test and homework answers.

Then there was Stacey, the thickest of the bunch. She carried it well, squeezing all of her 160 pounds into a size eight, always wearing clothes that complemented her body type. Stacey was pretty quiet but would quickly put you in your place if you stepped out of line.

Last but not least there was Wanda. If there was anybody that could give Brooklyn a run for her money in the looks department it was her. Wanda stood about five foot seven and had the perfect Coke-bottle figure. She was blessed at fifteen with a D cup and a round ass that any teenager and man alike would salivate over. In addition to beauty, Wanda had the voice of an angel, and her smile was contagious. Whenever there was a disagreement, she could always work her magic and straighten things out.

This group of girls was known as the PYT's, "pretty young thangs," and to say that they were popular would be an understatement. Every boy fell at their feet, and every female stayed out of their way.

This particular day wasn't much different than any other for the group, apart from getting to accompany each other to class for the entire day. It was career day, and each student was allowed to choose three careers of most interest. The PYT's chose law, medicine, and fashion, which were just checks on the sheet of paper they'd signed in on, because the interest just wasn't there.

The day had gone by swiftly. The girls were headed to the last class of the day when Brooklyn spotted Sincere, her longtime crush. Sincere was one of those guys that almost mesmerized anyone in his presence. He had graduated from high school a few years earlier, but regularly hung outside of the school or in the hallways until he was shooed away by one of the hall monitors. Sincere had a reputation in the neighborhood and with the ladies as being a "bad boy." His occupation of choice was drug dealing, and though he had a main girlfriend, time and time again you'd catch him sporting a different one on his arm. It was that bad-boy charm that attracted Brooklyn, who looked forward to getting a glimpse of him at least once or twice a day.

As the girls strolled in the direction of their class, Brooklyn stopped in her tracks and held a steady eye on Sincere, who stood near the end of the hall chatting with a few of his associates and admirers.

As Rene and Stacey walked into the room, Brooklyn tapped Wanda on the shoulder and nodded in Sincere's direction.

"Girl, I don't know why you won't go talk to him. He knows you want him." Wanda laughed.

"Because I don't chase them, they chase me. When are you going to learn?" Brooklyn smiled and shook her head. She wanted to run over and tell him how she felt, but that wasn't a part of her game. She told herself that she had to relax if she wanted things to go her way. "I mean, he needs to drop that chick, Maxine, if he wants me anyway," she blurted out.

"Maxine? He's still with her?" Wanda questioned with raised eyebrows. "Girl, you're going to have to stake your claim. Obviously she has something that he wants."

"Well, we both know it ain't looks." Brooklyn burst into laughter, and Wanda joined in as they both headed into the class. Brooklyn glanced at Sincere once more before going into the room. He smiled at her briefly before turning his attention back toward his conversation.

For Brooklyn, Sincere was perfect in every sense of the word. From his smooth, dark, mocha-colored skin to his pearly white teeth, he was the man she dreamed of being with. His hair was always perfectly cut, every strand obediently tamed, and with his attire, he always looked as if he'd stepped right off a designer advertisement. He wasn't particularly nice to anyone, especially the females he dated, but Brooklyn loved a challenge. She knew, if given the chance, she could change him for the better. She was confident that she had the ability to make any man melt in her hand, even someone as rough as Sincere.

"Young lady, could you come in and close the door please," the woman in front of the class called out.

Brooklyn was so wrapped up staring at Sincere, she didn't even hear the bell ring, or notice that her friends were already seated inside. They all giggled when she closed the door and came in. She flagged them as she headed to her seat.

Brooklyn's attention was now focused on the woman standing in front of the class. She immediately noticed how beautiful she was. Even dressed down, she looked like a supermodel, tall and thin with great teeth and skin. Brooklyn was captivated and found it almost impossible to take her attention off the woman. She'd been told most of her teenage years that she could be a model, but it never interested her—until now. She was more into scoring the boy she wanted and maintaining her reputation.

As Mesa stood confident in the front of the room and began her speech on fashion and modeling, Rene blurted out, "So where are we going this weekend? I heard the skating rink is going to be packed." Once she noticed that Brooklyn wasn't paying attention to her, she leaned forward in her seat and waved her hand in front of her face. "Brook, is anybody home?"

"What?" she snapped. "I'm trying to listen here."

The girls all turned to look over at her, disbelief splattered across all of their faces. Paying attention in class wasn't something that Brooklyn normally did. But they all knew not to fool with her when she was focused on anything, regardless of how silly it might seem to them. So instead of probing her, they continued the conversation amongst themselves.

Brooklyn, unfazed by annoying them, was still glued to the beautiful structure in front of the chalkboard behind the teacher's desk. The glamour was turning her on almost as much as Sincere did. She had to find out more about this profession and how she could get in.

Mesa Grimes, the twenty-something-year-old model, had made it in the business with not only her looks, but her wit and charm, all of which Brooklyn possessed. It was a known fact that Brooklyn stood out like a sore thumb. She was extremely confident, smart, and had the gift of gab. Sometimes her confidence could be misunderstood as arrogance, but everyone who knew her well normally overlooked it. Unknown to Brooklyn, Mesa was just as enthralled with her.

As Mesa spoke, it was almost as if she was directing all of her attention to Brooklyn, probably because she was the only one who seemed interested, but the truth was, Brooklyn had caught her attention from the moment she walked into the room.

Once the hour was up, the students in the class ran toward the door, almost knocking each other over. Brooklyn thought the chances of a girl like her from the ghetto turning into a supermodel were slim to none. She quickly refocused on the upcoming weekend and was telling the girls how great the skating party sounded.

As they neared the door, Brooklyn felt a tap on her shoulder.

"Do you have a few minutes to talk?" Mesa asked as Brooklyn turned around.

She was hesitant but told the girls to go ahead without her and she'd meet up with them outside of the building.

"Sure, I can talk. What about?"

"I noticed how interested you were in what I was saying. Have you ever thought about modeling?"

"Me? Yeah, right." Brooklyn burst into laughter. "In my world, shit like that doesn't happen. Excuse my French, but I'm just being real."

"Well, it's possible. You definitely have the look and the personality."

Confused, Brooklyn looked herself up and down. Though she always wore designer clothing, her wardrobe was always closer to a boy's than a girl's. She'd rock a tight fitted shirt but over it would be a loose jumper, and a pair of Adidas on her feet. Today her attire wasn't much different. She wore a pair of stonewashed jeans, grey flats with a few studs sporadically placed on both sides, and a loose white boat neck shirt that hung off her left shoulder. Her wrists were covered with bracelets that made a jangling noise every time she moved. She knew she looked good, but she couldn't understand where Mesa saw that model quality.

"Well, look—Here's my card and an application packet. If you're interested, we'd love to have you on our team. We are one of the largest independent modeling agencies in Philadelphia. We're actually an imprint of a much larger company in New York City."

Brooklyn stood there amazed. Things like that just didn't happen. She was the product of a broken home with a lush for a mother, and they lived in a neighborhood full of hustlers and drug addicts. *Is this really happening?* she thought. *She couldn't really be offering me a modeling contract.*

"I'm not pressuring you. Just take it home and have your parents look it over with you. Then we can set up a meeting to go over everything together. Deal?"

"Deal," she responded with a smile.

After taking the packet from Mesa, Brooklyn stuffed it into her bag before leaving the room. One thing she hated was people all up in her business.

She walked over to her friends, who were waiting for her at the end of the hall.

"I thought I said wait outside." She placed her hands on her hips and balled her face up.

Wanda spoke up for the group. "It's too damn hot outside. What's the big deal anyway? We weren't trying to be nosy, if that's what you think. We know how you are about your privacy."

"All right. Well, let's get out of here. It's the weekend, ladies. We need to go out and celebrate."

They all cheered and headed out of the building.

Brooklyn noticed Sincere standing off to the side of the street, leaning against his car. She gave him a flirtatious smile and waved at him. He returned the smile but tried not to make it too obvious, since Maxine was standing only a few feet away from him.

Maxine was one of the biggest troublemakers in the school. She and Brooklyn had come pretty close to blows on many occasions, but somehow, they were always separated and never made contact. Brooklyn felt like making her way over to Sincere. She didn't care about Maxine's presence and was pretty much ready for whatever she'd throw her way.

The girls followed behind Brooklyn as she switched over to where he was posted. He got up from the car as she got closer.

"What's up, Sincere?" Brooklyn smiled. "You're looking good today as always."

"It ain't nothing. I'm just relaxing. What's up with you?"

"On my way home to get ready for this party later on. I just wanted to come over and say hi."

"What party are you going to? I may swing by, since you're going to be in the building." He smiled.

"The party at the skating rink. Everybody is going. I hear it's going to be packed."

"Cool. I'll try and—"

"You'll try and what?" Maxine blurted out. She'd switched over once she noticed them having a conversation.

"Nothing, Max. I was just leaving. Don't worry. No one's trying to step on your toes."

"Whatever. You're like a stray dog, so I don't trust you. You'll screw anything!" she yelled.

"*Whatever* is right, sweetie. You have a good day," Brooklyn said. "Sincere, you do the same." Brooklyn turned to walk away, furious inside. *A stray dog?* She hadn't even had sex yet, so she definitely didn't appreciate being compared to a loose dog.

Brooklyn wanted to be the bigger person at that moment and ignore Maxine. She knew eventually they would come to blows, and planned to get a punch in for every slick thing she'd ever said to her. She quickly shook the thoughts of Maxine and walked along with her friends, discussing what they planned to wear that night. Brooklyn was excited and wanted to be sexy, just in case Sincere decided to swing by.

Once Brooklyn got home, her mother was on the sofa asleep, most likely sleeping off the effects of a long night of partying, so she sat the packet down on the coffee table in front of her and went up to her room. It was hard for Brooklyn to get her mother to focus on anything that didn't involve alcohol and partying. Fortunately, she had learned how to take on the responsibility of taking care of herself and her two younger brothers. Otherwise, things would have been in shambles years earlier. She knew the packet would probably lie there untouched for days, but she wanted to see exactly what could happen with it, figuring it was at least worth the try.

You never get anywhere in life sitting around waiting for things to happen, she thought.

She ran into her room and immediately began going through her closet. After pulling piles of clothing out onto the bed, she finally settled on the perfect outfit, a pair of straight-legged stonewashed jeans, a black tank top with thin straps, and a pair of black flat shoes. She rarely wore shoes, but she felt that this day was different. She was trying to impress Sincere, and with the clothing, her long hair freshly wrapped, and a little makeup, she was sure to blow him away.

Eight o'clock couldn't come fast enough for her. She was so excited, she had to lie down for a nap, just to make time go by. "Tonight is the night," she whispered to herself. No more playing around for her.

Chapter Two

Truly Sincere
1985

The music was blasting as Brooklyn and her girls entered the party. Teenagers were everywhere inside Carmen's Skating Rink, some skating, some playing the arcade games, others posted up in various areas, trying to get their mack on. They all headed straight for the counter to pick up their skates. Brooklyn loved to skate and was pretty good at it. She was one for showing off, doing tricks on the floor, getting all of the attention. Her friends normally were there to cheer her on.

"Size?" the guy at the counter yelled over the loud music.

"Two sevens, a nine, and a six and a half, please," Brooklyn shouted back.

He returned a few seconds later with all of their skates. They walked over to the chairs next to the lockers to put them on. Brooklyn continued to look all around the building.

Stacey noticed and questioned her. "What the hell are you looking for? Or, should I say, who, for that matter?" She laughed.

"I'm looking for Sincere. I was hoping he'd be here by now."

"Girl, you know how guys like him are. It wouldn't be right if he didn't make a grand entrance." Stacey laughed.

"Yeah, that's true. I'm really hoping he shows." Brooklyn blushed. Her stomach was all in knots as she continued surveillance of the room.

"He will, girl. Stop tripping. Let's get out here and have some fun!" Wanda stood up from her seat and began making her way over to the locker to put her sneakers inside.

Brooklyn laughed the comment off, though deep down inside she was about to burst from all of the anxiety.

"Let's go!" Stacey came over and pulled Brooklyn from the seat.

She got up and within minutes was focusing on showing off on the floor. Everyone was cheering her on as she flew around the rink doing dance moves and tricks good enough for a competition. As the center of attention, she was in her element, and so were her girls, who followed behind her. They soon grabbed onto her waist and formed a line to do their routine. Their favorite song to jam to was playing, "Roxanne, Roxanne" by U.T.F.O. The melody meshed perfectly with their moves.

Brooklyn was leading the pack, singing along, when she felt the hands behind her replaced by a larger pair. The hand switch was followed by a whisper in her ear.

"You're looking good tonight. I'm glad I decided to stop by."

She quickly turned her head and saw Sincere behind her. She couldn't stop blushing for a second. She almost stopped dead in her tracks, which could have sent the ten people behind her tumbling to the floor, but she focused and kept up the pace.

"I bet you didn't think I'd show up."

"No, I knew you would. I just thought you'd have a tagalong," she said with confidence.

Sincere burst into laughter. He loved her attitude. That had him drawn to her like a magnet. He laughed because he knew exactly who she was talking about, and in a way it was true. Maxine was definitely one that liked to hang on his arm every chance she got.

"I know you've heard that saying—Don't bring sand to the beach. I came here because I wanted to spend some time with you."

By now, the group behind them had dispersed to different areas of the floor. Sincere was still skating behind her, his hands firmly gripping her waist.

"Spend time with me? Why? You hardly pay me any attention."

"That's not true at all. I pay close attention. Shit!" Sincere snickered as he looked her up and down. "I can tell you everything you had on this week."

Brooklyn smiled and again couldn't contain her blushing. One of the most popular guys around had actually been checking her out. For the past year, all she could focus on was him. This day was like a dream come true. She could barely think of what to say next without sounding like a child.

"That's pretty funny. I never thought you'd be a stalker," she replied after a few seconds of contemplating what to say. She laughed.

Sincere joined in the laughter as he slowed down and began pulling her off the floor and over to the tables, where they sat down across from each other, both still smiling.

"So you know you're going to be mine, right?" He sat up.

"Who said that?" she replied, with a girlish grin and a giggle.

"I did."

"What about Maxine? That is your girl, right?"

"She is, but I'll drop her in a heartbeat for you."

Brooklyn sat there stunned. *At least he is being honest about Maxine,* she thought. She knew it wouldn't be that easy though. Maxine wasn't going to just accept that, and if being with Sincere was what she wanted, she'd definitely have to fight for him.

"So what if I said OK right now, would you drop her?"

"I just said I would, so does that mean you're mine?"

"That means I'll be yours when you get rid of her."

Sincere smiled, pausing to take it all in. He'd been after her for so long, but he also knew it was going to be hard to get rid of Maxine. The feelings he once had for her had long disappeared. Brooklyn was special, and now that he had a chance, he wasn't about to let it slip by.

Finally, after a minute he said, "I'm going to do that, for sure."

Rene and Wanda were on their way over to the table area to break up the conversation that was keeping their ringleader away. Still on skates, they startled Sincere and Brooklyn when they bumped into the table.

"Sorry to break up this little union here, but we need our girl," Wanda yelled, placing her hands on the table to brace herself from falling.

Sincere laughed. "It's cool. We'll have plenty of time to spend together, so I'll let her go for now."

"Well, excuse me, Mr. Sincere. I hope you live up to your name. If you hurt my girl, we'll have to kill you." Rene smiled, her left hand on her hip. Just then, she noticed Maxine walking toward the table. "Let's go. The wicked *bitch* of the west is on her way over here," she said, just before pulling Brooklyn out of her seat.

"I promise it won't be long," Sincere whispered as Brooklyn and her friends skated away. He couldn't take his eyes off her, even as Maxine walked up and stood in front of him, trying to block his view.

"What were you doing talking to her?" she asked, continuing to move her head in front of his every time he tried to get a glimpse of Brooklyn.

From the distance Brooklyn was looking back at him and smiling, confident he was going to do as he'd promised.

"What? I'm a grown-ass man, Maxine. I can talk to who I damn well please."

"I'm aware of that, but you're my man, so I want to know why the hell you're all up in her face?"

Sincere looked at her, his face twisted in a knot. He wanted to just get it over with and drop her at that point, but he knew the outcome wouldn't be good for any of them, including Brooklyn, and he was trying to avoid bringing drama her way.

Maxine stood there, waiting for his answer, hand on her hip and tapping her foot against the ground.

"Let's drop this before it gets out of control. I came here to have fun, and that's what I intend to do." Sincere began skating away from her, gently pushing her out of the way as he passed her.

"Sin, don't walk away from me," she yelled over the loud music. "I'm not done talking."

But Sincere skated away unfazed by any of the obscenities she yelled. Eventually she'd give up, like every other time he'd ignored her after a disagreement.

Maxine stood there getting angrier by the second as she watched him talking to Brooklyn yet again. They stood there laughing and giggling as she stood in the distance with the screw face.

"So what happened over there? I see your girl's standing there upset." Brooklyn knew what she wanted, but she wasn't in the mood to fight that night. She just wanted to know what the hell had her so upset.

"Nothing. She's always angry, especially when I'm talking to someone else, but I'm a grown-ass man." He laughed.

Brooklyn joined in the laughter while still looking over in Maxine's direction.

"Anyway, I'm about to bounce up out of here. I just wanted to come say good-bye before I left."

"Well, that was pretty thoughtful." Brooklyn smiled.

"I'm going to make good on that promise too. Just give me a little time."

"I'm patient, and I'll be here." She reached out and touched the back of his hand.

Sincere smiled before moving toward the lockers to retrieve his sneakers and return his skates. Brooklyn stared at him until he left the building. She turned around with the same huge smile on her face, but it quickly turned to a frown as Maxine and her crew approached her.

"Look, bitch, I don't know what you're trying to pull, but Sincere is mine. He's not going anywhere, so you need to get that through your head," she said, pointing in Brooklyn's face.

Brooklyn could feel the heat rising in her body as she tried to refrain from knocking Maxine upside her head. "Listen, if you have a problem, Sincere is who you need to straighten it out with."

"No, my problem is with you. You think you can just walk up and steal my man from right under me?"

"I'm not going to sit here and argue with you, Maxine. I have to go."

"I'm not done talking." Maxine blocked Brooklyn's path.

Brooklyn's friends noticed the commotion and quickly ran over to cover her. Once Maxine and her followers noticed they were outnumbered, they began to disperse.

"This ain't over, bitch!" Maxine spat. "Not by a long shot!"

Brooklyn thanked her girlfriends for responding when they did. That night they left the party without any more drama and caught the bus home. She was exhausted both mentally and physically by the time she reached her room. It had been an eventful evening. She was happy, though. For once, she could go to bed with Sincere on her mind, knowing that soon they'd be together.

Chapter Three

Touchdown
1985

"Mom, did you get a chance to look at that packet I left on the table a couple of days ago?" Brooklyn asked as she ran into the kitchen to get a bowl of cereal before heading out to school.

"What packet?" she asked, hungover from the night before.

Brooklyn's mom had just got in the house a few hours earlier after a long night of clubbing. Half of her body hung off the sofa, with one shoe on, and she reeked of alcohol.

"For the modeling agency. I need you to look it over and sign off on it," Brooklyn replied, annoyed.

"Modeling? Girl, how you gonna model, walking around here dressed like a boy? Don't make me laugh." Janice flagged Brooklyn and laughed as she got up from the sofa. Though she didn't spend much time with her daughter, she did know her taste in clothing, and no way did it resemble that of a model.

"Mom, I'm serious. The woman from the agency believes I have a lot of potential."

"Don't let them sell you a dream. You can't believe everything that comes out of someone's mouth, especially someone you don't even know." She lit a cigarette and took a seat at the kitchen table.

"Mom, could you just sign it please. It's something I want to do. I mean, I could be out in the streets doing drugs and God knows what else, but I'm trying to do something with myself. I thought I'd have your support." Brooklyn took a seat at the table and began eating her bowl of Frosted Flakes.

"Support? Don't come talking to me about support. Tell that shit to your deadbeat-ass father. I'm the one keeping a roof over your head. Matter fact, go see if you can find his ass and get him to sign your little permission slip or whatever the hell it is." Janice walked out of the kitchen still mumbling about support.

Nothing was ever easy with Janice. A permanent bar-hopper at night, most of the time she was either hungover or asleep. She worked as a barmaid at most of the neighborhood bars, and when she wasn't working, she would pull up a stool or hit the dance floor with a drink in her hand. Most days Brooklyn and her brothers didn't see her. They'd gotten so used to it, they stopped complaining about it. Brooklyn had to become the mother around the house, cooking, cleaning, and doing the laundry or anything else her mother was slacking at.

Brooklyn hadn't seen her father John in years, but shit, she barely saw her mother and they lived under the same roof. She was only five the last time she'd seen her father and remembers that day as if it'd just occurred. He hadn't said good-bye and never even bothered to reach out to her.

It didn't take long before her mother met Bill, who'd later become the father of her younger brothers, Kevin and Jason. Bill turned out to be an abusive alcoholic, who Janice finally kicked to the curb after years of being punched and kicked herself. Unfortunately for Brooklyn and her siblings, now nine and eleven, Janice picked up the drinking habit that she once despised. She couldn't count on both hands the number of times her mother lay pissy drunk on the living room sofa or floor and she'd get her changed and up in the bed before her brothers could witness it.

From the outside looking in, some would say Brooklyn and her two brothers had it made. They always wore name-brand clothing, thanks to the boosters who would stop by and drop off clothing that Janice had either paid or done favors for. They always had a full refrigerator, courtesy of their corner store credit, and their house was fully furnished with expensive furniture that her mother of course got on a discount. At least she was good for something, Brooklyn would always say, even when she was pissed at her.

It was times like these when their neighbor, Ms. Rose, came in handy. Ms. Rose, in her fifties, was one of those women who felt the need to take care of other people's children when their parents weren't around. And Janice didn't disapprove. So whenever Brooklyn needed a parent to go up to the school for a meeting or to sign a permission slip and her mother was unavailable, she'd run over to Ms. Rose.

After eating and hollering up to Kevin and Jason to get up for school, Brooklyn grabbed her things and headed across the street to Ms. Rose's house. As usual, she was wide-awake and making breakfast for whoever stopped by before school to grab a plate. Brooklyn could smell the aroma of bacon as soon as she walked in the door.

"Morning, Brooklyn." Ms. Rose smiled as she opened the door and walked back toward the kitchen. "Did you eat yet? Breakfast is almost done."

"Yes, I ate already. I came by to see if you could sign this packet for me."

"What's it for? You know I don't just sign my name on anything." She laughed.

"It's for a modeling agency. They came to the school for career day, and the woman wants to give me a shot. She thinks I have potential."

"That's great, darling. Sure, I'll sign it for you. Anything that'll get you out of this neighborhood, I'm all for it. I believe you have the potential to do anything that you put your mind to."

"Thanks so much!" Brooklyn ran over to hug Ms. Rose, nearly knocking her over. "You're always there when I need you to be."

"Well, just don't forget about me when you hit it big." Ms. Rose laughed.

"I could never forget about you!" Brooklyn smiled. "I'm going to run. I don't want to be late."

"OK. Let me know how things turn out," Ms. Rose replied, retrieving the last bit of bacon from the frying pan. Ms. Rose took pride in caring for others. She'd lost her own son in a car accident, and after years of depression, she found that giving support to the children in the neighborhood was the closest she'd ever come to being a mother again.

Brooklyn, already out of the kitchen and almost through the front door, was so excited, she couldn't wait to drop off the packet at the counselor's office. She was so focused on getting herself a modeling gig, she didn't even stop by Stacey's house to meet the girls to walk together. By the time she realized that she'd forgotten, she was a block away from school. She ran into the building and straight to Ms. Thomas' office with the packet in hand.

"Good morning, Brooklyn. What can I do for you today?" Ms. Thomas asked with a smile.

"I have to get this packet to Mesa Grimes from the modeling agency."

"OK. Well, you can leave it here with me, and I'll make sure that she gets it."

"Thanks." Brooklyn turned to leave the office.

"Brooklyn," Ms. Thomas called out, "what made you want to get into modeling? I never thought you'd be into something like that."

"I never thought I would either, but she believes in me, so I'm going to give it a shot," Brooklyn replied with confidence before turning and leaving the room.

Ms. Thomas picked up the phone and dialed the agency number that Mesa had left the previous week. She was well aware of Mesa's confidence in Brooklyn, and although she'd never mentioned modeling to her, she always knew she was a star. Mesa was excited and promised to pick up the forms later on that day.

Brooklyn hurried to class but was caught in the hallway by her girlfriends, who were all pretty annoyed that she hadn't waited for them so that they could all come to school together as they normally did.

"I thought that you must've been sick or dead," Stacey yelled. "Why didn't you tell us you were coming to school early? We were almost late waiting on you, until I called Ms. Rose and found out that you left early."

The others nodded their heads in agreement.

"I'm so sorry. I had a meeting with the counselor this morning that I couldn't miss," she lied. "Besides, it's not like you've never left me before."

"Let's get to class before we're all late," Rene blurted out, trying to defuse the situation before things got out of hand.

Growing up, Stacey and Brooklyn had always been as close as sisters, but just like sisters, they occasionally had fights. Sometimes the fights would end with a friendly hug, but there were other times when they came close to an all-out hair-pulling brawl. Most people thought that their bumping heads was inevitable, since the two were so much alike.

Brooklyn and Stacey stood there staring at each other, both waiting for the other to speak or make a move. Rene and Wanda, used to their antics, decided to just walk away, knowing they'd follow suit. Rene took the first step and headed toward her class at the end of the hall. After Wanda headed up the stairs, she looked back to see the two of them still standing there.

Stacey, arms folded and lips pouted, said, "I hope this doesn't have anything to do with Sincere."

"It doesn't. I already told you I had to meet with the counselor."

Deep down Stacey was jealous of Brooklyn and Sincere. She'd never been lucky enough to catch the interest of a man like him. Regardless of how cute she dressed or how perfectly her makeup was applied, it just wasn't enough. Besides that, she didn't want to lose her friend. She knew that without Brooklyn by her side, she'd lose the shine that kept her in the limelight.

Brooklyn nudged Stacey on the shoulder and laughed. "Don't worry. No one's taking me away. Even if I snag Sincere, you'll still be my girl!"

Stacey laughed, though inside she wasn't laughing at all. She knew what would happen once she got with Sincere. It would be just a matter of time before she made herself scarce from the group.

"Now let's get to class. We're late!" Brooklyn grabbed Stacey by the arm and walked down the hall.

As they walked past the staircase, Stacey glanced to her left and saw Wanda still standing there. Wanda gave her a slight smile, and when that smile wasn't returned, she knew things were headed in the wrong direction. She turned and walked up the stairs, her mind focused on fixing whatever the problem was.

Brooklyn was floating on cloud nine, thinking about getting her shot at modeling. She didn't even notice that Stacey was still down. They entered first period and sat down next to each other, as they normally did.

"Glad you ladies decided to attend," Ms. Brooks called out from the front of the class.

"Sorry. I had to meet with the counselor," Brooklyn responded.

Ms. Brooks turned her attention back to the board and began her lesson.

The day for the girls turned out to be a typical one, until the school bell rang at 3:15. Brooklyn walked out of the classroom and hurried toward the front door. She didn't see her friends but figured they'd most likely be waiting on the opposite side of the door. She pushed open the large doors, and instead of seeing her friends, she saw Maxine with two other girls standing off to the side of the gate. She wasn't concerned, because she knew Maxine wasn't bold enough to try something with her friends close by.

Brooklyn continued to canvass the area and still didn't spot her friends. She decided to head home, but Maxine and her crew stopped her. They instantly began a staring match.

"Can I help you?" Brooklyn broke the silence while still holding her stare.

"Actually you can. You can start by leaving my man the hell alone," Maxine yelled, moving closer to Brooklyn.

"Girl, first of all, you need to tell your man to back away from me, if that's the issue. Your man is after me."

"He's only after you because he thinks it's pissing me off," Maxine said, both hands on her hips and her face twisted in knots.

"Obviously, it's working because—"

Before Brooklyn could finish the sentence, Maxine's fist met the right side of her jaw.

"Bitch, are you crazy?!" Brooklyn yelled between clenched teeth as she lunged at Maxine's neck and began to choke her.

Maxine grabbed hold of Brooklyn's wrists, trying to loosen her grip, but was unsuccessful as Brooklyn's combination of anger and adrenaline made her much stronger. Maxine's group of friends, who were standing off to the side cheering her on, were now assisting in the attack, pulling Brooklyn's hair and clothing to release the hold.

"Get off of her!" one of Maxine's friends yelled, referring to the grip Brooklyn had on Maxine's hair.

Brooklyn refused to let go. She began punching Maxine, vowing to at least give one of the three girls a beating before they got the better of her. The fight lasted about five minutes before she heard Sincere's voice and felt the girls backing away one by one.

"So you're going to take up for that bitch?" Maxine yelled while Brooklyn tried to get one last hit in.

"Go home, Maxine. You're acting real childish. You think this will make me come back to you? Well, think again! I told you last night we were over, and I meant it!"

"You don't mean that," she cried, trying to reach in to hug him.

Sincere pulled his arm away from her and quickly gave her his back as he walked toward Brooklyn. Maxine stood there pouting for a few seconds before turning around and walking over to her friends.

Brooklyn was still standing there watching, her feet planted, ready for round two. Her hair was a mess, and her shirt was torn, but she didn't care. The adrenaline had her pumped.

"Are you OK?" Sincere lifted her chin to look at her lip, which she could feel swelling at that very moment.

"I'm good, but she better hope we don't run into each other anytime soon!" She screamed, still fired up.

Sincere smiled and grabbed her hand. "I'm going to take you home, OK?"

Brooklyn didn't respond as he wrapped his arm around her waist and led her to his black BMW. She was floating on air, loving the way his hand felt against her body, which was now starting to ache from the punches she'd just received. She was smiling from ear to ear as they got in and drove away, leaving Maxine standing in the dust with her face twisted. Though she was pissed about the attack, being with Sincere was just the payback she deserved, and she was ready to get the show on the road.

Maxine put her middle finger up at Brooklyn as the car drove by, and Brooklyn looked at her with a silent laugh and waved good-bye, pissing her off even more. She smiled as she looked back over to her left at Sincere, who was bobbing his head to the music playing on the radio. Even with all of the drama, Brooklyn couldn't have asked for a better end to her day.

At that moment, "Sucker MC's" by Run-D.M.C. was the only thing on Sincere's mind. Maxine was simply a thing of the past.

Chapter Four

Battle between Friends
1985

Brooklyn decided to head out to school early. She wasn't in the mood to be bothered with Stacey and wanted to avoid the confrontation she knew would eventually happen. She was still angry that her friends hadn't been there for her the day before when she fought with Maxine. As she headed in the direction of school, all sorts of things cruised around in her mind. She wondered how her friends could be so jealous of what she had that they would leave her stranded knowing that Maxine would attack the moment she was alone. She also thought about Sincere and the fact that, with all of the drama, she'd finally achieved the one thing she wanted for so long. She had Sincere all to herself.

She reached the corner of the school when she heard her name being called. The voice was all too familiar, and instead of carrying a happy tune, it was loud and angry.

"Brooklyn, I know you hear me!" Stacey yelled as she walked faster to reach where Brooklyn was standing.

Brooklyn turned around and huffed, "Yeah, I hear you, but I don't really care to listen to what you have to say." She shook her head and put one hand on her hip.

"What the hell is your problem?"

"You're my problem, Stacey," she screamed and pointed in her direction. "You and your selfish attitude."

"How am I selfish?" she replied, shocked by the comment.

"You know exactly what I'm talking about. If you weren't so busy acting like a jealous bitch, things would be fine. But, no, you can't stand to be happy for me. You can't stand that I got the man that everyone wishes they could have."

"Jealous? Brooklyn, don't kid yourself. I have nothing to be jealous of. Ever since you got your little modeling contract, you think your shit doesn't stink. Well, let me tell you one thing—Don't be so sure you'll keep him. He'll drop your ass the same way he dropped Maxine."

Brooklyn laughed. "You are so pathetic, Stacey. It kills you to see me doing better than you."

"You know what, Brooklyn . . . I'm not going to stand here and argue with you any longer. It's not even worth my energy. Just remember the next time you're getting your ass beat or when you're alone after he dumps your ass that you could've had friends to lean on."

Brooklyn stood there unfazed as Stacey brushed past her and walked across the street and into the school. Maybe she was a little hard on Stacey, but she hadn't found a way to forgive her. And she believed that since she was with Sincere, she wouldn't need friends. She walked into the school a few minutes later and went through her day without much conversation with anyone.

Anxious to get out and hoping to see Sincere waiting for her, Brooklyn exited the building at three o'clock to find that he wasn't there. Instead of looking around for him and risk being embarrassed, she began to walk home. Soon she heard her name being called. It turned out to be Sincere.

"Why are you walking home? I can't have my girl walking around with sore feet, not when I have this nice-ass ride." Sincere smiled as he walked around the car, which was double parked near where Brooklyn was standing.

"I wasn't sure if you were coming, and I didn't want to look like a fool standing out there waiting."

"Come one now. I would never have you looking like a fool. Matter fact, I'd prefer if you looked like new money." He reached into his pocket and pulled out a wad of money. Then he peeled off three hundred-dollar bills and placed it in Brooklyn's hand.

"What's this for?" She looked down at the crisp bills in the palm of her hand.

"Just like I said, I want you to look like new money, so that means take that money and buy you something nice. There's plenty more where that came from."

"Sincere, I can't take this money."

"Why not? You're going to hurt my feelings if you reject my gift."

"I'm definitely not trying to hurt your feelings, Sincere. It just feels weird to be taking this kind of money from anyone, that's all."

"Well, I'm not just anyone, Brooklyn. I'm your man." He moved close to her and wrapped his arms around her waist.

Brooklyn's stomach was doing flips as she felt the heat of his body next to hers.

"Now, I need you to put that money away, hop in the car, and let me take you home. Could you do that for me?" He smiled.

Brooklyn stood there feeling like a kid in a candy store. She knew there wasn't any point in debating with him. He kissed her softly on the forehead, backed away, grabbed her by the hand, and led her to the passenger side of the car. She got inside and watched Sincere walk around to the driver's side, a huge smile on his face.

He got inside and looked over at her before grabbing her hand. "Don't be afraid, all right. I promised you that we would be together, and we are. I don't need you chickening out on me. That's the only way this thing is going to work."

"I won't."

He turned on the music and began to drive off. At that moment she was reassured that things between them would only grow from that point. She couldn't let the words that Stacey shouted earlier that day mess up a good thing. She believed that this relationship and her modeling career were the blessings she needed.

Once they pulled up in front of her house, he kissed her on the cheek and gave her a hug before she walked into the house floating on cloud nine.

Brooklyn's smile was turned upside down as soon as she opened the door and found her mother standing in the hallway with her hands on her hips and her face twisted.

"Who the hell was that dropping you off, with your fast ass?"

"That was just a friend from school, Mom."

"Friend from school, my ass. Last time I checked, teenagers weren't driving around in BMWs. Do I look like a fool to you?"

"No, Mom, you don't."

"Well, I know one thing. If you're going to be giving your time to some nigga and missing doing your chores and shit around here, you better make sure his ass give you some money. We could use some things around here. Do you hear me?" Janice yelled, waving her hands in front of Brooklyn's face as she stood day-dreaming.

"I hear you, Mom."

Janice turned back around and walked into the living room. It was just like her to turn the tables and try to make things work in her favor.

Rubbing her hands across the pocket that contained the money Sincere had just given her, Brooklyn debated if she should reveal it to her mother. After a few moments of pondering, she decided to pull out a hundred dollars. Without a word, she walked into the living room, placed the money on the coffee table, and turned to head up to her room. Then she quietly retreated to her bedroom, where she spent the rest of her evening looking forward to the future.

Janice looked down at the money on the table and quickly scooped it up and placed it inside of her bra.

Chapter Five

Rock Steady
1985

"Come on. I need your help to pick out the perfect outfit!" Brooklyn pulled Wanda up the stairs in her house toward her bedroom. She and Sincere had a date that evening, and she wanted to make sure everything was perfect.

Two weeks had passed since the fight with Maxine, which was also the beginning of the relationship between her and Sincere. With Sincere constantly working, they hadn't had an official date yet. On occasions like these, when trying to make an important decision, Brooklyn always enlisted the help of Wanda, the most practical of her friends, and to Brooklyn, this was almost the most important decision she would make. She had finally snagged the man of her dreams, and right from under Maxine's nose at that.

Brooklyn laid out different styles of jeans on her bed and pulled out random shirts from her closet. "Come on, Wanda, help me. Aren't you happy for me?"

"To be honest, no, I'm not. He's ruined our friendships. I just want things to go back to the way they were."

"Correction—Stacey ruined our friendship by acting like a jealous bitch, not Sincere. And, furthermore, me and you will always be friends. Nothing will change that. When she should've been happy for me, she was angry that I wanted to be with my man instead of playing childish games with her. I just need you to support me like a true friend, though, and help me pick out something to wear. You know how important this is to me." Brooklyn pouted, trying to win her longtime friend over.

Wanda sat, knowing that things would never be the same but still hoping that they would be. Instead of ruining her friendship with Brooklyn, she decided to help her and be as supportive as she could be without Stacey's knowledge. With Brooklyn missing from their pack, Stacey had taken the reins as the leader of the pack, and Wanda didn't have what it took to stand alone.

"All right, all right. Let's see what we have here. You have to be sexy if you're going to keep Sincere's attention." She smiled and started grabbing clothing off the bed, holding them up in the air to get a better look at them.

Brooklyn settled on a pair of straight-legged, stone-washed jeans with flat shoes, and a screen-printed T-shirt. Her accessories were loaded with tons of bracelets, headbands to match, and huge earrings. She applied minimal makeup, hoping to appeal to him by keeping as much resemblance as possible to her normal appearance. She didn't want to overdo it and totally turn him off.

After Wanda wished her good luck and hugged her good-bye, Brooklyn's nerves started to get the better of her as she waited for him. Twenty minutes past the appointed time, she was pacing the floor, hoping he wasn't standing her up, and peeking through the curtains every few seconds just to see if he had pulled up and she didn't hear him. She'd look like a fool for dissing her friends all week if he didn't show up.

"He'll be here," she said aloud, trying to stop herself from getting upset. "I know it. He wouldn't stand me up. I just know it."

Meanwhile, Sincere was in his car on the west side of Philadelphia, hurrying to drop off one of his lady friends. He looked down at his watch and realized he was twenty minutes late to pick Brooklyn up. He should have turned down the erotic invitation, but good sex was hard to come by, and Octavia, an older woman, knew how to please. He kept looking down at his watch every few seconds.

"Don't worry. You're so smooth, you can talk your way out of anything. I'm sure your explanation will satisfy her." Octavia smiled.

"Maybe," he replied, not so sure that it would. Not too familiar with Brooklyn's ways, he didn't know how she'd react to his tardiness.

Oddly, Sincere had an understanding with all of the women he dealt with on the side, all of them aware that they weren't his number one. So Octavia, being one of those women, knew she had to stay in her place if she wanted to keep seeing him on a regular basis, as she had been for the past six months. After dropping her off at home, he quickly gave her a kiss on the cheek and made his way to North Philly to pick up Brooklyn.

As he pulled up in front of Brooklyn's door, he beeped the horn and parked. After a minute or so, he got out of the car and knocked on the door when she didn't appear.

Brooklyn sat there on the sofa, peeking out of the window. She laughed as she watched him walk to the door. She was going to make him work after making her sit there dressed to impress for over a half-hour.

After she heard a knock, she took her time walking to the door and opening it. She stood there, her face twisted in knots, waiting for him to say something.

"I'm sorry, OK. I know I'm late as hell, but my brother had an emergency that I had to help him with. I really didn't mean to keep you waiting."

"I'm gonna let you slide this time, but please don't make a habit of it." Brooklyn smiled, closing the door shut and coming out on the top steps. With her brothers asleep and her mother out working, her night appeared to be going as planned, except for the delay.

"You look good as usual."

"Thanks. So where are we going?"

"To the movies. *Krush Groove* is playing. Then we can probably grab something to eat, if it's not too late."

"OK."

They walked toward his car, where he opened the door for her and allowed her to comfortably sit down before closing it.

They arrived at the Sam Eric in Center City twenty minutes later, just in time for the movie. The theater was flooded with teens and adults alike, all wanting to see the hip hop-inspired film, featuring rappers like LL Cool J, Kurtis Blow, and Run-D.M.C. It seemed like almost everyone greeted Sincere, who was one of the most successful young drug dealers in the city. Along with his older brother, he was unstoppable. Brooklyn proudly hung on his arm as they made their way to the seats in the rear of the theater.

Most of the moviegoers were laughing, talking, and throwing popcorn throughout the theater, even during the opening credits, but the moment Run-D.M.C. began to rap "Sucker MC's" in the booth with the red light shining on the dimly lit studio, the crowd went wild. Even Sincere was out of his seat, rapping along with the duo as they jammed on the screen.

Brooklyn enjoyed the movie, but being with Sincere was the real prize. He paraded her around for at least a half-hour after the movie was over as they hung out in the lobby of the theater. Passersby watched with envy the two beautiful people who appeared to mesh so well together.

After leaving they decided to go grab some pizza and hang out for a while before he took her home. He was anxious to get to know more about the girl who was pretty radiant and mysterious at the same time.

They sat down at the table with slices of pizza, talking and laughing, enjoying each other.

"So tell me more about you. I want to get to know everything I can about Ms. Brooklyn." He laughed before taking a sip of his soda fountain Coke.

"Well, I like fashion, hanging out with my friends, and skating, I don't really do much else."

He laughed as he noticed just how young she actually was. He knew the number, but knowing the things she enjoyed really confirmed it. "Well, we're gonna have to change that, you know. If you're gonna be with me, no more being a kid. You have to be a woman. Sincere doesn't date chicks who act like children."

Brooklyn ate some of her food and then took a sip of her soda, trying to let what he'd just said sink in. *What did he mean by that?* she thought. "I'm really mature for my age. Everyone tells me that," she replied confidently, sitting up taller in her chair.

"Yeah? Well, what do you sleep in when you go to bed?"

"That's a little personal, don't you think?"

"Not at all. We're trying to get to know each other. You just said you were mature, so act like. I didn't ask what was under what you sleep in. I already know that, baby. I've seen plenty of naked bodies."

At first disturbed by his reply, she had to think again before responding. She didn't want to appear childish but as if she knew it all. "Well, I sleep in nightgowns mostly, if you must know."

He laughed but quickly followed up with his next question, which was sure to make her even more uncomfortable. "So are you a virgin?"

"As a matter of fact, I am. I haven't had many boyfriends, and the ones I had weren't worth giving it to."

Surprised that she answered without hesitation, he replied, "Wow! Didn't expect that answer."

"Why not? Do I look like a whore or something?" she asked, a little annoyed.

Sincere burst into laughter. "Now if I thought you were a whore, I wouldn't be caught dead with you on my arm. I'd never take you out with me in the streets. So, no, I don't think you're a whore. I think you're beautiful."

Brooklyn began to blush. He knew just the right thing to say at just the right time. "So what made you want to get with me, Sincere? Really? I'm not fast or anything. I know you have plenty of girls at your beck and call."

"Honestly, I saw something special. And, sure, I do have access to other women, but they aren't important. They are disposable like perishables."

"So how do I know that you won't say the same thing about me?"

"Have some confidence in a brother." Sincere laughed, and Brooklyn joined in the laughter.

They continued to eat their food and talk for what seemed like hours before Brooklyn realized how fast the time had gone by. She had to get home to make sure her brothers had eaten dinner and hadn't torn the house to shreds. Since it was Friday, she was positive that her mother would be out drinking and partying.

Sincere was satisfied with their date and was happy to take her home at that moment. Before she stepped out of the car, he grabbed her by the arm. She wasn't ready to kiss him but knew that she would if he asked.

"I really enjoyed our time together, and I want you to be my girl. I want to give you the world because you deserve it. I mean that, OK."

"I really enjoyed our night out as well, Sincere. Thanks a lot."

"Well, before you go, take this money and go shopping on me tomorrow. Get you some new gear. Not that I don't like your style, but the tomboy stuff has to go. I need my girl looking like a lady." Sincere went in his pocket and pulled out two hundred dollars and passed it to her.

She wasn't comfortable taking that much money from him but she didn't want to upset him by not taking it. She thought about what he'd said, and if looking like a lady was what he wanted, she was surely going to give it to him.

He reached over and gave her hug before she got out of the car. After opening her door, she blew him a kiss good night. He smiled and drove off.

Chapter Six

Mr. Loverman
1985

It was almost 7:45 A.M., and Brooklyn and her brothers were in the kitchen scrounging around for a suitable breakfast so they could make it in time for school, which began at eight o'clock.

"Stop making all that goddamn noise!" Janice yelled, rubbing her forehead. She tried to shield her eyes from the sunlight poking through the window, as she lay on the sofa nursing a hangover. As usual, she'd come in so drunk, she couldn't make it up to her bedroom.

"Look, we'll get something from the corner store because we're all gonna be late for school." Brooklyn tugged at Kevin, the older of the two, causing him to slip out of the chair. His face was balled up as he looked over at his brother, whose smile had also turned into a frown.

The boys got up with sad faces and growling stomachs. They hadn't eaten dinner the night before because their mother was out clubbing and Brooklyn was out spending quality time with her new boyfriend, Sincere. For the past week the boys had noticed Brooklyn's absence since no one was there to make sure they had what they needed, including food and beverages. If it weren't for running water, they probably wouldn't have had even a drop of liquid to quench their thirst.

Brooklyn continued to push them toward the door, grabbing their coats and school bags on the way.

"I'm hungry, Brooklyn," Kevin yelled as he neared the door. "We've been missing dinner every night!" He stopped walking and turned to Brooklyn.

"I know, Kevin. I'm sorry. I'll make sure I'm here tonight to cook, OK, but right now we have to go. You can grab anything from the store, even junk food, if you want." Brooklyn smiled as she pushed them out the door.

Kevin smiled back. They had both missed her, though Jason was too young to express it.

Brooklyn walked them to the store and spent some of the money Sincere had given her the night before. After leaving the store, they headed their separate ways toward their schools. Waving good-bye, she smiled at them, even as she felt an urge to do more for them.

As Brooklyn walked toward the building, she heard someone calling her name. It turned out to be Stacey. She hadn't spoken to her since Maxine and her friends had jumped her. She was still angry that they weren't there to help her out. Brooklyn acted as if she didn't hear her, as Stacey yelled louder, almost loud enough to be heard from five city blocks away.

Stacey was out of breath by the time she got to where Brooklyn was standing. "I know you heard me," she said, hands on her hips.

"What's up?" Brooklyn replied, ignoring the comment.

"I've been trying to catch up with you. You've been missing in action since you and Sincere got together."

"That ain't true. I still live on Styles Street. You know where to find me."

"Why the attitude, Brooklyn? Did I do something to you that I'm not aware of?"

"Are you serious? Don't you remember? I got my ass beat because you weren't around."

"You can't blame that on me. I've always had your back. Maybe if you'd stop chasing a man that's already attached, you wouldn't have that problem." Stacey was pissed that Brooklyn was accusing her of not being there for her when she'd been there for her every time she'd needed her. She'd even been the one to sneak food out of her own house to help Brooklyn and her brothers when their party-animal mother neglected to feed them. Here she was, standing in front of the most ungrateful person she'd ever laid eyes on. It almost made her sick to her stomach. Stacey stood bracing herself for Brooklyn's response. If she knew anything about her friend, she knew she wouldn't let that comment go without a comeback.

"No. If *you* weren't acting like a jealous bitch, it wouldn't have happened," she hollered, her hand in Stacey's face.

Stacey, visibly offended, didn't reply but instead brushed past Brooklyn and headed toward the school. Brooklyn wasn't fazed. She didn't give a damn about her attitude or her friendship at that point. A true friend would love the fact that she'd finally gotten the man she wanted. A true friend would have also been there to have her back, knowing full well Maxine and her friends would attack her the moment they saw her alone.

After standing there for a few seconds watching Stacey walk up the street, Brooklyn continued on the same route in the direction of the school. She entered the building alone that day and watched as her friends gave her the evil eye before going into class.

One of the girls, Wanda, displayed a looked of sadness. She hated that their group was being separated.

Things hadn't been the same in the past few weeks, and she didn't know if they would ever be. Wanda waved to Brooklyn as she walked behind Stacey, hoping to be unnoticed. For the moment, Stacey was the leader of their pack. Wanda wondered if Sincere was truly the cause of the drama, or if there was something much deeper going on between the two that she wasn't aware of.

Brooklyn began slowly walking to class when she heard Ms. Thomas, the counselor, calling her name.

"Hi, Brooklyn." Ms. Thomas motioned for Brooklyn to come over to the office. "Just wanted to give you a number. Mesa from the modeling agency has been trying to reach you, but your home phone is disconnected."

As usual Brooklyn's mother hadn't paid the bill, so their service had been cut. She could have been missing the opportunity of a lifetime because her mother was more interested in partying than taking care of her responsibilities.

"So sorry. My mom must've forgotten to pay the bill," she replied, making excuses for her mother. "I will call her today. Thank you so much for the information."

"No problem. Just be sure to call. She's really interested in you." Ms. Thomas smiled as she passed Brooklyn a late pass. "Here, you'll need this."

Brooklyn went to class the remainder of the day thinking only about modeling, envisioning runways and photo shoots, meeting tons of celebrities, and wearing expensive clothing. She desperately wanted to get out of the situation she was in, to be able to take care of her brothers and not have to depend on other people. Not even Sincere crossed her mind that day. Of course, he could take care of her, but she was tired of using others as a crutch.

The day seemed especially long, so eager was she to make that phone call. Once the bell rang, she ran out of the building but stopped in her tracks after noticing Sincere posted in his usual spot off to the side of the building. She strolled over to him, a big smile on her face.

"Hey, baby. I see you got on that new dress I bought you. Looks good. I love to see my money spent well." Sincere smiled, grabbing Brooklyn around the waist and pulling her in for an embrace. He got a whiff of her Chanel No. 9 perfume as he kissed her on her neck.

The students in front of the school focused on the picture-perfect couple as they stood next to one another.

"You better stop giving me so much affection, or I won't be able to resist stripping your clothes off and kissing you all over."

Backing away but still remaining flirtatious, Brooklyn was smiling from ear to ear. She could feel his eyes tracing her slender figure. "Well, you're going to have to. Besides, you wouldn't do that in front of a crowd of people, would you?"

"Shit! Doubt me if you want." Sincere laughed. "I'll have you butt naked on the hood of the BMW."

They both burst into laughter, imagining the sight.

Though Sincere had been extremely patient with Brooklyn being a virgin and hadn't pressed the issue, Brooklyn was aware that eventually she'd either be forced to give it up or he'd move on.

"Where were you in a rush to?" Sincere had noticed her running out of the building and was interested in knowing what was so important that she almost didn't notice him standing outside waiting on her.

"I need to make it to a phone. I have a very important phone call to make. I was on my way over to Ms. Rose's house." She fixed her schoolbag, which had fallen off her shoulder.

"We can go to my house, and you can use mine." Sincere stood up from his seated position on the hood of the car.

"I can't stay tonight, Sin. The boys haven't eaten dinner all week, so I have to stay home with them and cook. I'm really sorry. I'll just use Ms. Rose's phone, and I'll see you in the morning."

"So that means I have to sleep alone? I thought you were staying over tonight?" He pouted, hoping to get her to change her mind.

At least twice a week Brooklyn would spend the night when her mother was working at the bar. It wasn't truly a big deal, since he'd be sure to use the free time wisely and call up one of his female friends to warm his bed all night long. Sincere liked Brooklyn. A lot. She was beautiful, and she was pure, both of which made him more anxious to be deep inside her virgin walls. On the nights that she slept next to him, he'd pull the sheets off her, revealing her half-naked body, and as she lay oblivious to his thoughts and movements, he'd reach into his boxers, pull out his rock-hard dick, and stroke it until he'd come in his hand. He wanted to taste her just as much as he wanted to eat food when he was hungry, but he believed this was the start of more than just a sexual affair.

"Babe, I'm really sorry." She began backing away from him.

"No problem. Be careful going home. Call me if you need anything." He leaned in to kiss her before releasing his grasp on her hands.

Sincere watched her walk away, and as soon as she was out of sight, he signaled to Allison, who was standing against the wall near the corner store.

Allison jumped at the chance to go home with Sincere, even if it meant she'd be invisible to him the next day. For that moment, and at least the remainder of the night, she'd feel like she was his girl. As she walked over to him, she fixed her dress over her thin frame and ran her fingers through her hair, trying to look perfect for him. She stopped in the same spot where Brooklyn had stood only moments earlier.

"Can I help you?" she asked, sticking her ass out just enough to arouse his senses.

"You definitely can help me. Question is, do you want to?" Sincere grabbed his crotch, as he looked her up and down.

She tried to keep a straight face though she wanted to jump on him and stick her tongue down his throat. She held it together long enough to reply, "No question."

"Well, hop in, so we can go to my place and make some magic." Sincere opened the passenger-side door to his car and motioned with his hands for her to get inside.

As she walked around the car and sat down in the seat, he took a quick surveillance of the area. Confident that none of Brooklyn's friends saw Allison get inside, he closed the door with a devilish grin and walked around to the driver's side. Once he got behind the wheel, he looked over to his right, rubbed his hands together, similar to a criminal with a master plan, turned his key in the ignition, adjusted his radio, and pulled out of the parking spot. Allison waved to her circle of friends, who'd been watching the entire time. Within a few seconds the black BMW turned the corner and disappeared from view.

Chapter Seven

The Usual Suspects
1986

Three weeks later, things at home for Brooklyn and her brothers weren't much different. Their mother was still noticeably absent. A week prior she'd come home with some news to share with her family. Though interesting, the news didn't surprise Brooklyn at all. In fact it annoyed her. Janice, the alcoholic absentee mother of three, had gotten married. Always spontaneous and known to make bad choices, lately her choices had been borderline crazy. She'd met Fred at The Big Moose, the local bar that was always packed with patrons, where you could count on never finding an empty seat, even during the day.

Normally, you'd find Brooklyn pulling her brothers away from the door as they bent down on their knees, trying to avoid being seen, as they stole glances of their mother's activities. Janice would be so caught up, she wouldn't even notice them.

Fred didn't even appear to be the marrying type, but for some reason, Janice's view was clouded. He was unemployed, his teeth were rotten, and he reeked of cigars and alcohol. In front of the patrons of the bar, he'd asked her to marry him, and her response was "Let's do it now!" The next day they went down to City Hall without any of their families present and tied the knot. Brooklyn and her brothers were shocked when she came home dressed in her Sunday best, her new husband hanging on her arm.

"Kids!" she hollered through the house.

Brooklyn could tell by the raspy tone in her mother's voice that she was drunk. *It's four o'clock in the afternoon,* she thought. *She's starting earlier and earlier every day.*

The boys were in their room playing with their race cars while Brooklyn cleaned up the kitchen to prepare their dinner. She didn't budge when she heard the annoying scream from the front door.

"Kids! I know you hear me. Get your asses down here! I have a surprise!" she yelled as she moved into the living room with Fred by her side.

Brooklyn could hear the boys running down the stairs and into the living room. She casually strolled in a few moments later. "Will this take long? Because I have to get dinner started."

Brooklyn was even more annoyed when she saw Fred standing there smiling, dressed in a pimp's suit, his shoes shiny, and his pants creased so hard, they looked like they could stand up on their own. Something about him rubbed her the wrong way, but she couldn't put her finger on it at that moment.

"Fix your goddamn attitude, Brooklyn. I am your damn mother. I called you all in here to make an announcement. I would like you to meet Fred. Fred, there are my spoiled-ass kids!" Janice laughed. "Kids, this is your new father. We just got married today."

Brooklyn rolled her eyes and sucked her teeth. *Married? She could not be serious,* she thought. There was no way in hell she was going to call his pervert-looking ass "Daddy."

Fred looked Brooklyn up and down when he noticed her attitude. It was a typical reaction, as far as he was concerned, but he didn't care whether they liked him or not.

"Can I go now?" Brooklyn asked with attitude. She had heard and seen enough.

"No, that's not it. I also wanted to tell you that I'll be spending a lot more time over his house, so you're going to have to step up and take care of the boys on the nights I am away.

"I do that anyway," she responded, rolling her eyes. She wasn't upset, she actually enjoyed the days her mother wasn't around. She had more peace when she didn't have to hear her hollering and screaming, or help her out of her pissy clothes when she'd come in drunk as all hell.

"Keep it up, Brooklyn, and you're going to get the shit smacked out of you! Matter fact, go ahead and get the hell out of here. I'm sick of looking at you."

Brooklyn mumbled under her breath as she left the living room and walked back toward the kitchen. She wasn't afraid of her mother but didn't want to fight in front of the boys. Always prepared for a fight, she would have slapped her ass right back. She knew it was wrong to fight one's parents but felt like her mother didn't have the right to discipline them when she didn't even raise them. The only time she wanted to act like a parent was in front of other people, so they wouldn't look at her like the deadbeat she was. Brooklyn didn't want to leave her brothers, but she knew it was just a matter of time before she left them behind.

She stood in the kitchen annoyed as she prepared dinner. She could hearing Janice and Fred laughing and joking in the living room as if they'd been together for years. Just before dinner was done, the couple left the house without a word. Brooklyn was relieved.

After they ate dinner, she helped Kevin and Jason get washed for bed then ran across the street to Ms. Rose's house to call Sincere. She needed to hear his voice before going to bed, especially after the news she'd just heard.

Sincere was lying across his sofa while Allison was on her knees, giving him the best head he'd ever had. Lately, she'd been fulfilling his needs when it was too hard to resist Brooklyn. He had waited patiently as long as he could, but his patience was slowly running out. He looked down at Allison as she looked up at him, and their eyes locked. He'd trained her well. At sixteen she was doing more than most of the adult women he'd been with. He only dealt with her because she was na-ïve. He knew she wouldn't risk losing him by running to Brooklyn, so he used her as often as he could. But, in reality, he could've cared less about her. Girls like Allison were disposable, but girls like Brooklyn came once in a lifetime. Every time Allison looked at him, he pictured Brooklyn, anticipating the day when she'd be here instead.

Sincere closed his eyes as Alison's wet mouth cov-ered his pulsing head, one hand stroking his shaft, the other massaging his balls. He could only let out a sigh as he fought back an early eruption.

He grabbed hold of her long, black ponytail and pushed himself deeper inside of her mouth, almost tickling the back of her throat. She would gag each time he thrust deeper, but she refused to ruin it. She didn't want him to think she couldn't handle it.

Sincere pulled her up and instructed her to turn around. Resting her elbows on the arm of the sofa, and sticking her ass up in his direction, he got behind her and slowly guided his dick deep inside her tight teen-age pussy.

Allison instantly let out a sigh as he filled every inch of her. She bit her bottom lip, trying to ignore the pain. Her young body wasn't used to the force of a man, but she tried her best to fake it.

Sincere continued to pound her from behind until he neared an eruption and quickly withdrew himself from inside her and released his juices on the small of her back. As he sat down on the sofa and wiped the sweat from his forehead, Allison got up and headed to the bathroom to clean herself up.

Just as she left the room, the telephone rang. He reached over to the end table to answer it.

"Hello," he said and cleared his throat.

"Hey, Sin. It's Brooklyn."

Sincere was surprised that she was calling so late. "Hey, what's going on?"

"Just wanted to hear your voice, that's all."

"You sure?"

"Well, not really. My mom just pissed me off. She just got married to some nigga she don't even know then came in here parading him around. I'm just so annoyed."

"You want to come over?"

Allison caught a whiff of the conversation as she entered the room and was instantly annoyed. Feeling disrespected after having given him her body just a few moments earlier, she walked over and attempted to kiss Sincere, who pushed her away. She sucked her teeth loud enough for Brooklyn to hear through the phone. Sincere gave her a look of death, and she backed away, sat down on the chair and began to put on her shoes.

"No, I don't want to be a bother," Brooklyn said. "Besides, I don't want to leave the boys tonight. I'll just see you tomorrow." She really didn't want to leave them or end up fighting the female she'd just heard in the background. Keeping her cool, she finished her good-bye, saying, "Just come get me after school, OK."

"OK, I'll be there."

As soon as Sincere hung the phone up, he jumped up and grabbed Allison around her neck. "Listen, bitch, just because I have sex with you from time to time doesn't mean you're my girl. You fuck things up with Brooklyn, and you'll regret it."

Sincere's eyes were bulging, and spit flew from his mouth as he screamed in anger. He had always been able to control his women, but Allison for some reason appeared to be slipping.

She was pulling at his hands as she fought to breathe, tears coming out of her eyes and her light skin turning beet-red.

"Do you understand me?" he yelled.

After he let her go, she began to cough uncontrollably and rub her neck, which was throbbing with pain. She wanted to run out of the house and scream for help, but that would only make things worse. She sat up on the edge of the sofa and continued to cry.

Sincere looked over at her and began to feel sorry for what he'd just done. He didn't intend to hurt her, but he wasn't about to let anyone ruin what he had with Brooklyn. He walked over to where she was seated and attempted to console her, placing his hand on her shoulder, but she jumped as soon as she felt his touch.

"Look, baby, I'm not going to hurt you, OK."

She looked up at him with puppy dog eyes. The man she once admired had showed her a side of him she hated. She was fighting with herself because she didn't know whether to love him or throw something at him. As she stared at him, she thought about all the things he'd bought her, name-brand shoes, bamboo earrings, and two-finger rings. She constantly had money in her pockets, and when he could, he would take her out to dinner and movies. There wasn't a boy in school who could afford to do that for her. She knew he didn't love her and that she'd never mean as much to him as his precious Brooklyn, but number two was better than nothing at all. If she didn't do as he asked, she'd lose it all, and at this point, that wasn't an option for her.

See, Allison was a beautiful girl, but growing up, she'd never felt like she would ever be noticed. Her father had been absent most of her life, and her front door was revolving with men constantly coming in and out, keeping her mother's bed warm most evenings. If there was one thing she learned from her mother, it was this—To pay the bills, sometimes you had to lay on your back, spread-eagled.

Allison didn't have the skills that most girls did at her age, and she also wasn't good at dressing herself up to get noticed. It wasn't until her friend Jane showed her how to style her hair and wear makeup that she caught Sincere's eye. Now she sat here wondering, was it all worth it?

Just then her mother's voice played in the back of her mind. *"Do what you gotta do to keep money in your pockets."* At that moment she stood up, wiping the tears from her eyes, and kissed him.

He wrapped his arms around her and looked at her for a moment. "That's my girl," he whispered before kissing her again.

After dropping Allison off at home and giving her a hundred-dollar bill, Sincere headed over to the bar to check in with his elder brother Sidney, whom he idolized. Born to the same mother but different father, they looked just alike, and Sidney molded Sincere as they grew. You never saw one without the other, and if you fought one, you had to be ready to fight the other as well. The glamorous life was what they always dreamed of, and now they were living it.

Sid and Sin were the top drug duo this side of Philadelphia, and no one had the heart to test them or try to step into their territory. At the young age, Sincere had just as much if not more respect than his twenty-four-year-old brother, which told you that by the time he reached Sid's age he'd be unstoppable.

Sincere entered The Big Moose smiling and shaking hands with the patrons. He'd give the ladies hugs, smacking a few of them on the ass, and they'd turn and giggle. You wouldn't know that less than an hour ago he'd almost choked a female to death.

Sidney was sitting at his usual table toward the back with a glass of Southern Comfort in one hand and a Newport cigarette in the other. As he blew out smoke, Sincere sat down in the chair opposite him.

"What's up, li'l bro? I see you got the new sweats on, looking clean and shit." Sid laughed as he put his cigarette out in the ashtray.

"Yeah, you know me. Gotta stay fresh for the ladies."

"You know those ladies are gonna be your downfall." He continued to laugh.

"What the fuck you mean by that?"

"You always chasing them. You need to focus on this money."

"That's where you got me confused. I never chase no females, they chase me."

"Yeah, all right. Anyway, I need you to get up with me first thing in the morning to make a run, all right."

"All right." Sincere glanced over at two men who were looking at him suspiciously. He could tell he was the topic of their discussion. He tried to keep his cool because the owner of the bar was a friend of theirs, but he would tear the place up in a heartbeat if a nigga got out of line. The two men tried not to look obvious once they noticed Sincere was staring back at them.

Sidney noticed the look on Sincere's face. "What's wrong with you?"

"These two clowns over there at the bar are talking about me, and I'm about to go find out what the hell the problem is."

"Come on, Sin. Calm down." Sidney tried to reason with him. "You can't go fighting every nigga that looks your way. You gonna get killed."

"Naw. I just want to go see if I can help them with something, that's all." He slid his chair out from the table and began to get up.

"Sin, don't start no shit. I don't feel like this tonight."

Sincere smiled as he stood and walked over to the two men, who were now looking in his direction.

"What's up, gentlemen? Is there something I can help you with?"

The darker of the two, seated farther from Sincere, said loudly over the music, "What?"

"You were looking in my direction as if you were discussing me. I figured I might as well come over and help you with the correct answers, you know."

"Actually, it was your girl we were discussing, not you, my man."

"My girl? And who might that be?" By this time, Sincere had his fist balled at his side.

"The chick, Brooklyn. I was just telling him how she has the sweetest ass this side of North Philly." The darker one laughed as he tapped his friend on the shoulder.

Everyone in the neighborhood knew that Brooklyn was Sincere's girl. He often paraded her around like a trophy, just in case anyone had any doubt.

"Oh really?"

Sidney could see Sincere's anger from across the room. He gulped the last bit of his drink before standing to walk over, but just as he stood up, Sincere hit one of the guys, knocking him off the bar stool, and followed up by stomping him as he tried to get up from the floor. The friend, who was attempting to hit Sincere from behind, didn't notice Sidney coming and was hit across the back of the head with a bottle, which instantly knocked him out cold.

As patrons of the bar scattered, knocking drinks and tables over, Sincere and Sidney stomped on the two men until they were no longer moving and left them bloody and unconscious in a fetal position on the concrete floor.

Sidney tossed two hundred dollars on the bar to cover the damage as the owner cursed them both. Once he and Sincere made it outside, they jumped into Sincere's car and drove off. Sincere began laughing hysterically, while Sidney sat furious in the passenger seat. He hated attention. No matter how much he tried to talk sense into him, it seemed to go in one ear and out the other.

Sincere straightened out when he noticed his brother wasn't participating in the laughter.

Sidney turned to look at him, almost ready to hit him. He was tired of getting into street brawls for no reason. "Man, what the fuck is your problem?"

"Man, that nigga straight up disrespected me, talking 'bout my girl and shit. I'm not going to have that, Sid. You seen how he was looking at me. I go over, and he saying how she's a sweet piece of ass."

"So all of that over a bitch, Sin? Come on now. Use your fucking head. How you know that nigga wasn't lying? And even if he was, she's the person you need to be mad at, not that nigga. I don't get you, man. You're gonna fuck around and get hurt one of these days, man. I love you, but I'm not always gonna be there to save your ass." Sidney turned to look out of the window. He was hoping that Sincere was really listening to what he was saying.

"First off, Brooklyn isn't like these other bitches. I mean, she's the one I'd marry, man. That shit hurt, man. How would you feel if a nigga said that they fucked your wife?" He waited for a response, but Sidney didn't answer or even turn to face him. "I mean, I get it. I'm damn sure gonna say something to her, to make sure she ain't lying to me. She told me she was a virgin and shit, so if I find out that's not the truth, she will look like the rest of these tramps to me. But until then she means so much more, Sid."

"I get that you care about the shorty, but you can't go fighting every nigga that says he tapped that. I'm your big brother, and I love you, so I don't want nothing to happen to you. We're doing too good for this shit to fall apart, especially over some female."

"All right, Sid. I'll get it together." Sincere knew full well, if put in the same situation, he'd react the same exact way. He hated his brother to be angry with him, though; he was all that he had, so for now, he'd say whatever he had to for him to drop it.

"All right, cool. Run me home. I'll get Jax to drive me back to my ride later."

The remainder of the ride was silent, both of their minds in different directions. Sincere planned to stop by Brooklyn's that evening and get to the bottom of the situation that weighed so heavily on him at that moment. What bothered him the most was that he had been such a gentleman and respected her wishes to wait for sex, not attempting even once. He'd been showering her with expensive gifts and keeping her pockets filled with cash, not expecting anything in return. But, as a man, you can only be denied sex for so long, and to hear that she'd possibly given it to someone else, all the while lying, saying she was a virgin, infuriated him to a breaking point. There was no way he could go one more day and not address it.

After he dropped Sidney off, he drove straight to Brooklyn's house. Confident that her mother wouldn't be home, he knocked on the door. He knew she'd be surprised to see him.

After a few knocks, Brooklyn came to the door, calling out from behind the rugged wooden frame. "Who is it?"

"It's Sin, Brooklyn," he replied in his smooth tone. "Open the door."

Opening the door, she smiled, tugging at her pink bathrobe to make sure no part of her body was sticking out. "What are you doing here?"

"I missed you, that's all. Can I come in?"

"Sure, come on." She looked up and down the block to make sure no one saw him enter. She was in no mood to fight with her mother about having him in the house when she wasn't home. For sure she'd be called every slut in the book if caught.

Sincere walked up behind her as she walked toward the steps and hugged her from behind. He was trying to make her feel comfortable enough to get up to her bedroom.

She let out a girlish giggle and pushed his hands away as he tried to move them under her robe. "What are you doing?" She laughed.

"Just trying to see what you have on, that's all," he lied.

They entered her bedroom, which had teddy bears lined up on a shelf on her wall. Pink sheets and posters of random celebrities lined her walls. By the looks of the room one would think a much younger girl slept there, all of which should have been clues of her honesty.

As she sat down on the edge of the bed, Sincere sat down next to her and began to stare at her so deep, it made her uncomfortable. Blushing, she turned away, hoping to break his stare.

"Look at me," he said, reaching in his pocket for some candy.

"No, I can't, because you're staring at me."

He laughed. "I won't stare at you. I just want to give you something I brought you."

"What is it?" She turned immediately.

"It's just some candy. I know it's your favorite."

She burst into laughter as she grabbed the chocolate candy from his hand. She opened up a few pieces and ate them, unaware they were laced with "special *k*," a street drug.

Sincere, still upset about the information he'd heard in the bar, was anxious to get to the bottom of things. His face was now serious. "So I have something to ask you, and I really need you to be honest with me, OK."

"I'm always honest with you, Sincere. Ask me anything."

"When you told me you were a virgin, were you being honest with me?" He rubbed his hands through her hair softly, trying to make her feel comfortable.

"Of course. What made you ask me that?" Strangely, she was feeling lightheaded but still tried to stay focused on what he was asking her.

"Because today I heard otherwise, and I just want to know if I can trust you. Before today, I did, but now I'm not so sure," he said, his tone now stern, the softness disappearing as he noticed she was appearing drowsy and less focused with each passing second.

"Who would tell you something like that? I haven't even had"—Brooklyn fell down onto the bed unable to move, her eyes still open.

Sincere sat for a moment pondering his next move. He knew it would alter their relationship, but he couldn't go any longer without knowing whether or not she was honest. He untied her robe, revealing her pink nightgown underneath. He reached under the nightgown and pulled down her panties to face her nakedness for the first time. For a second he thought about turning around and walking out of the door, leaving her untouched. No real man would rape his girl and risk taking her virginity just to find out if she was a virgin in the first place.

He quickly pulled down his pants, letting them drop to his ankles, and spread her legs far enough. Being so close to her almost made him erupt and he didn't even touch her. He grabbed his dick, which was hard as a brick, and slowly guided it inside of her. Though her walls were extremely tight, he still wasn't certain.

He saw a tear streaming down the side of her face and wanted to stop, but he was feeling too good to pull out now. In fact, he picked up the pace and began using more force, moving in and out, as he ignored her pain. Her pussy wrapped around his dick so tight, it was almost smothering it. He stopped when he felt like she was too wet. After pulling out, he noticed some spots of blood on the bed underneath her.

Sincere felt like the biggest asshole on the planet for what he'd just done. Instead of her enjoying her first experience, she'd know that she was raped. He stood up and pulled his pants back up. He began pacing the floor, trying to figure out what to do. He thought, *Maybe she'd forget all about it, with the drugs and a good night's sleep.* He went into the bathroom and grabbed a washcloth. He wet it then went back into her room and tried to clean her now swelling lips. He put her panties back on and positioned her on the bed and pillow.

After kissing her on the forehead and whispering how sorry he was in her ear, he left the house unnoticed by her brothers. The entire ride home he thought about the fact that he hadn't thought things out, something Sidney had warned him about.

Chapter Eight

24 Karats
1986

Brooklyn smiled as she shook hands with Mesa Grimes. She'd just had her first meeting regarding the contract the agency had offered her. The following week she'd do her first test shoot to begin her portfolio. Mesa was almost as excited as Brooklyn.

Brooklyn's mind was focused on getting out of the ghetto, and moving on to bigger and better things. Now it was much more than a dream and more like a reality. She could imagine her face in the magazines and on billboards. She left the office with a new attitude, one that focused on her future and not on some of the negative things that weighed her down.

Brooklyn hadn't yet found a way to forgive Sincere. Ever since the night he had raped her, he'd been showering her with gifts, hoping to make up for what he'd done. She didn't give a shit about the clothes and fancy jewelry. What she did care about was, he'd robbed her of the one thing she'd held sacred. Though she still kept in touch with him, she hadn't spent the night with him or even let him get close enough to hug or kiss her, every encounter being uncomfortable for her. But keeping contact with him was a way to keep food coming in for her brothers, and she didn't want to risk throwing that away.

To make matters worse, she felt like she had no one to talk to. Since her argument with Stacey, the group of friends she once could call on was no longer within her reach. She missed them even more after that night, but she knew there wasn't any point in trying to reconcile, as long as she was still with Sincere.

Walking outside of the building, she put on her Gazelle's and ran her fingers through her hair. Then she adjusted her dress to make sure everything was in place. She walked over to the BMW, which was waiting for her with Sincere patiently sitting inside. She climbed in and sat quietly, not really in the mood to talk. Knowing he wouldn't let the entire car ride remain silent, she prepared herself for small talk.

"So how did it go, baby?" he said, placing his hand on her thigh.

Frowning, she looked down at his hand then up at him, and he removed his hand.

"It went fine."

"Just fine?"

"Yeah," she said as she turned to look out of the window, her mind wandering. She loved him, but she knew he was bad for her.

"Why the funky attitude, Brook? What's crawled up your ass and died?"

"Nothing, Sin. I just answered your question."

"You didn't answer my fuckin' question, you know. Why don't you stop being such a bitch all the time. There's plenty women that would love to take your place," he yelled, sick of getting the cold shoulder. Shit, if she didn't want to be with him, then she should have left a long time ago.

"Listen . . . stop threatening me. Because, if you wanted me gone, I would be gone."

Sincere wanted to wrap his hands around her throat or, better yet, smack the shit out of her for disrespecting him, but he held it together. Instead he probed her for the information he'd originally asked her. "So when are they going to start getting you work?"

She sat silent for a moment before answering, unaware of how close she came to being abused. "We do the test shoot next week, and hopefully, after that I'll start getting work."

"That's good. I'm happy for you. You really deserve the best."

"Thanks, Sin." She turned to him and smiled. She could appreciate him showing his compassionate side. When she fell in love with him, it was partly because of it. "So where are we going anyway?"

"I'm taking you somewhere special to celebrate your new contract." He laughed and patted her on the leg, drawing a smile from her. "Don't worry. I promise you'll enjoy it."

They drove to a French restaurant in Center City, Philadelphia. The valet took Sincere's car keys and gave him his ticket. They walked into the high-class establishment, which was full of older wealthy white couples.

The hostess looked at them strangely as she greeted them. In fact, they were the only young black couple in there. She was probably wondering how they could afford a meal worth one hundred dollars each. Immediately, she assumed he was drug dealer.

"Hello, and welcome to Le Bec-Fin. Do you have a reservation?" she asked from behind the wooden podium.

"Yes, two for Sincere Blake at six P.M."

"OK, I see you here. Follow me right this way," she said, directing them toward the main dining room.

***

Most of the patrons looked them up and down and whispered under their breath as they sat down. Brooklyn was smiling from ear to ear. She had never been in a restaurant nearly as nice as this one. The lighting was dim in the historical-looking building, which had large chandeliers hanging from its ceilings, and the tables were covered with white tablecloths. Hell, she hadn't even seen one on TV.

After getting glasses of water and ice tea poured, they looked over the menu, which included a variety of seafood and steak combinations that instantly caught her eye.

"This is really nice, Sin. You really didn't have to do this."

"Why not? You're my girl. I'd do anything for you."

She smiled, taking it all in. The little argument that they'd had in the car on the way over no longer mattered. He was definitely making up for his attitude.

"Look, I know I've done some fucked up things, and I can't take them back, but I plan to make up for them in any way I can, to show you that you're the one for me. I've never met a girl like you, and I truly let my inability to trust cloud my judgment. And I was wrong for that. I love you, and I hate that we argue so much now. I want to get back to the times when I made you smile. You think we can work on that?"

Brooklyn's body was warm. She wanted to jump over the table and kiss Sincere for taking responsibility for his mistakes.

She held in the laughter that almost burst out of her when he slid a little black box across the table. "What is this?" she asked, almost afraid to open it. He'd given her plenty of rings before but not after he'd poured his heart out.

"Just open it and see." He pushed it closer to her.

The waiter was now standing at the edge of the table. Looking down noticing the black box he asked them if they wanted more time. Sincere nodded.

Brooklyn grabbed the box and held it in her hand. *What the hell is he doing?* She thought. She was only sixteen, not nearly old enough to be married. Maybe she was overreacting, and marriage wasn't on his mind at all. Slowly she opened it to find a diamond ring. It appeared to be an engagement ring.

"Sin, what are you doing?"

"Look, it's just a promise ring. I know you can't really think about marriage at your age, and I understand that. So just take it, and promise me that, when you are a little older, you'll consider marrying me."

She didn't know what to say. She didn't want to say the wrong thing and ruin the nice evening he'd planned. *A promise couldn't be that bad. Hell, promises could be broken. Fuck it. I'll play along with it.* The ring was beautiful. Like nothing she'd ever seen. She slid it off the placeholder and put it on her finger. She held out her hand to see how it looked on her. It shined alongside the tennis bracelet he'd just bought her the week before.

"What am I going to do with you?" She shook her head and smiled.

"Just keep loving me and don't give up."

"I can do that."

The dinner was better than she expected. Seafood that tasted as fresh as if pulled out of the sea that day mixed with Sincere catering to her was the perfect combination. He was winning her back.

Following the dinner they headed over to his house, where he planned to just lay next to her and go to sleep.

But Brooklyn had plans of her own. She knew that if she didn't stop being afraid or uncomfortable around him, things would never progress, and she wasn't about to sit still.

The house was quiet as they entered, apart from the patter of the dog's feet. Butch, Sincere's black Doberman, was almost the same height as Brooklyn when he stood on his hind legs. He ran toward the door, practically tackling Sincere when he entered the foyer. Brooklyn, still a little bit afraid of the dog, stood near the door until Sincere calmed the dog down and took him into the kitchen for some food.

She walked over to his record player and shuffled through the records he had sitting off to the side. Spotting "Rock Me Tonight" by Freddie Jackson, she smiled. Here Sincere was this hard gangster type with love songs, but then she thought about how suave he was and knew they were only for the ladies.

This night, she planned to show him that she could move on and make the best of the situation. The fact of the matter was, outside of the rape, he was the best thing that had ever happened to her. She put the record on the turntable, placed the needle on to it, and pressed play. Soon the mellow sounds of Freddie's voice boomed through the speakers.

She began to remove her clothing, hurrying up, so she could sit down on the sofa and surprise him when he came back in.

Sincere entered the living room. "Hey, baby, I bought you some more"—He paused upon noticing her nude body. Instantly he turned around to avoid looking. "What are you doing, Brooklyn? You don't have to do anything. That's not why I gave you the ring," he said, his back still turned. He didn't know how to react, and assumed that getting too excited would ruin his chances of ever making her comfortable again.

"Sincere, turn around please." She giggled. She was now standing with her hands on her hips, revealing the full length of her body. She had never been more ready to be with him than she was at that moment.

"Brooklyn, I really want to, but I don't want to mess things up. We had a good night, and I want it to end that way." He stood still as a statue, holding two glasses of ice tea in his hands. He was never afraid to look at anyone; usually, he'd jump right on them. But Brooklyn meant so much more to him than a quick screw.

"Sit the glasses down and turn around, OK. You won't mess it up. Just a little while ago you said you would do anything for me, right?"

"I did say that but . . ." He felt her hands around his waist and instantly got a hard-on. His body was betraying him. He'd tried to hold back, but her touch made it virtually impossible. He could smell the scent of her perfume, Chanel No. 9, the scent that made him weak, the scent he couldn't resist taking a whiff of. Even if someone else was wearing it, he always thought of her.

"Sit the glasses down—now," she whispered into his ear as she pushed on his arms from behind him into the direction of the end table.

Finally, he obliged and took a deep breath before turning around and meeting her lips with his. He massaged her tongue with his, moaning as he did so. His body temperature was rising as his adrenaline began to pump in overdrive. He'd waited for this moment for so long. They both had, and now that it was happening, their hormones were going wild.

His hands were all over her, touching places he hadn't been able to touch before. Her body was soft as cotton, just as he'd imagined it would be. They continued to kiss each other as he led her to the sofa. Staring her in the eyes, he paused to stand and undress.

Brooklyn looked at his smooth, chocolate body, a sculpted masterpiece. She rubbed on his back as he got back in position on top of her and began kissing her neck. Inexperienced, she didn't know what else to do, but what she did know was, his kisses on her neck and body felt first-rate.

He paused again. "Are you sure you want to do this?"

Without a reply, she pulled him down and kissed him again, confirming that there wasn't any turning back.

Sincere slowly guided himself inside her womanhood, which welcomed him with lubrication and a tight grip. He continued with a slow thrust, moving in and out of her tunnel, all the while looking at her to make sure she showed no sign of pain.

She smiled and continued to kiss him, and they moaned in ecstasy.

"I love you, Sin," she whispered.

"I love you too." He'd never told her he loved her. He felt like he showed it often but was never able to allow himself to speak the words.

Within seconds, after confessing his love, he erupted. His body shook as he kissed her, and she held on tight. They lay there for some time before showering and going to bed both satisfied. Things from that point on would be much better between them.

Chapter Nine

Take a Picture
1986

"OK, now turn to your right . . . yes, just like that. Now smile," the photographer spoke in between snapshots of Brooklyn.

Inside the large studio located on Fourth and South Streets in South Philadelphia were Brooklyn, the photographer, his assistant, and another model, who was in the back preparing for her shoot. For the first time she was without a chaperone, since her agent was out of town this particular weekend.

Brooklyn had been featured in a few local magazines as well as one national magazine called *House of Couture*, in which she'd participated in a full six-page spread. She had also been invited to New York Fashion Week to walk the runway alongside two other models signed to the same agency. School, which she had since given up on, was the last thing on her mind. Modeling was all she could eat, sleep, or breathe at that point.

"OK, let's change for look two," the photographer said, calling for a break.

Brooklyn had been shooting for an hour straight and needed a break. She'd never realized how hard modeling was. When she entered the dressing room, Tania looked over at her.

"I'm Tania," she said, reaching her hand out to shake Brooklyn's. Tania was a few years older than Brooklyn and had been modeling for four years.

"Hi. I'm Brooklyn."

"You're doing good. Looks like you're a natural. Mesa is your agent, right?"

"Yes." Brooklyn was quickly changing into her next outfit as Tania sat looking into the mirror.

"Well, just a word of advice . . . don't let temptations ruin you."

Brooklyn looked over at her. "What do you mean by that?"

"I mean everything that can turn your life upside down. Men, drugs, and money, they will all ruin you if you allow them to."

"Well, thanks. But that won't happen to me," she said, confident she could handle herself in any situation.

"We all say that, Brooklyn, but the truth is, you are no match for sin. It'll make you think that it could change things for the better and end up turning your world upside down."

Though Brooklyn was a complete stranger, Tania felt compelled to speak a few words of wisdom. She reminded her of herself and the days before she wasn't an addict or suffering from an eating disorder as she tried to keep up with the younger females in the industry. She also knew that a hard head made a soft behind and hoped that Brooklyn would heed her warnings and avoid making some of the same mistakes that she did.

"Well, thanks again," Brooklyn said as she put on her shoes, "but I'll be OK. I'm sure of that." She gave a forced smile as she turned to walk out of the room, annoyed that a woman she didn't know from a can of paint was trying to tell her what to do. She believed that she would be able to manage anything thrown her way, and regardless of how naïve she appeared, she knew how to take care of herself, or at least she thought she did.

Once back on set, she began posing and smiling for the camera.

A few minutes into shooting, Sincere walked into the studio. Brooklyn had been there a little longer than expected, and it was just like him to become so impatient that he had to come inside to find out what the holdup was.

For a few weeks prior to this shoot Sincere had made sure to drop her off and pick her up on shoots or shows, claiming that he wanted to make sure that she arrived to and from safely. But Brooklyn knew that he had a much more sinister reason for hanging around. Sincere was definitely jealous of the attention she was receiving, and felt threatened by the photographers and other men who sometimes hung around the studios and events.

As Sincere stood off to the side, Brooklyn continued taking cues from the photographer, adding a sexy flair for Sincere to enjoy, but he didn't seem entertained. After a few more frames, the shoot was a wrap, and she ran over to Sincere to hug him.

"Go get dressed, so we can go," he said as he pushed her away.

"What's your problem?" she asked, not sure what the attitude was about.

"I got some place to be. Now hurry up. I'll be outside." He turned to walk toward the door.

Brooklyn stood there for a moment knowing that the look on her face would just embarrass her even more had the others occupying the room noticed. After a few seconds and deep breaths, she turned around and walked through the studio to gather her things. She threw her things into the bag without even folding or organizing them, anxious to see what was going on with Sincere and trying to avoid pissing him off any more.

"Remember what I said. If you don't believe me now, soon you will," Tania said as Brooklyn headed out of the room.

Brooklyn walked out of the studio and made it over to Sincere's car. As soon as she sat down, he reached over and smacked her, knocking her sunglasses off her face. She grabbed her cheek, which immediately started throbbing.

"Are you fucking him?" he yelled.

"Who are you talking about, Sincere?" she cried. She wasn't positive who he was referring to, but she knew she'd been faithful to him.

"That nigga in there taking the pictures," he screamed as he held onto the steering wheel with his left hand, keeping his right hand free, waiting for her to say the wrong thing so he could smack her again.

"No, Sincere. Why would you think that? I don't even know him."

"I saw you trying to be all sexy and shit. You think I didn't notice you showing off for that nigga?"

"I was being sexy for you, Sincere. That had nothing to do with him, or the photos for that matter."

"I must really look like an asshole, huh?" he yelled. He turned the car on and pulled out of the parking spot.

Sincere didn't really trust any woman because most of the women he'd encountered were either gold diggers just interested in his money, or liars who couldn't tell the truth if their life depended on it. Always feeling like they'd do anything to keep money coming in, he didn't see Brooklyn as the exception.

As they sat silent on the drive to her house, Brooklyn grabbed her compact mirror from her pocketbook and looked at her face, which had since turned red.

As soon as they pulled up, she reached for the door handle to exit, but Sincere grabbed hold of her left arm. "You're staying with me tonight, so go get some things and hurry up back out here."

She wanted to run in, lock the door, and hope that he wouldn't kick the door down to get inside, but she knew that would only make the situation worse. Normally, when he got this angry, he'd end up apologizing before the night was over. She just had to do everything he wanted her to do to keep him calm.

She didn't respond as he loosened the grip on her forearm, but nodded her head before getting out of the car. She wiped her face before unlocking the door, hoping to remove any sign of her tears.

The boys were sprawled out across the living room floor watching TV but quickly turned their attention to Brooklyn once she entered the room.

"Where's Mommy at?" she asked as she stood in the doorway.

"She's upstairs asleep. Are you staying home tonight?" Kevin asked.

"No, not tonight. I just came to get a few things and to make sure you two were OK. Did you eat? I figured she'd be drunk or missing in action."

"Yeah, we ate," he replied.

"OK. Well, call me at Sincere's if you need me." She headed toward the door.

Brooklyn hated leaving them so much, but being with Sincere and modeling took up pretty much all of her time. Her mother, who was rarely home on the evenings that she was out with Sincere, was often unaware of her whereabouts. Brooklyn always checked on her brothers but never had to explain anything to her mother. Before walking out of the door, she promised them that she'd stay home the following week.

After arriving at Sincere's house, she headed for the stairs.

"Go get cleaned up. I'll be up in a minute."

She was in no mood to have sex, but she was aware that if he wanted it she really didn't have a choice. She had so many things on her mind and wondered how things had gotten so messed up. There was a time when he worshiped the ground that she walked on, but now he'd knock her down any chance he got.

She turned to look at him, before taking another step, wishing he could be the man she fell in love with, but he had already turned and headed toward the kitchen. She hurried upstairs and jumped in the shower, hoping that he'd get so wrapped up in what he was doing, he'd forget all about having sex.

Unfortunately for her, he was in the room waiting when she came out of the bathroom. She instantly felt nauseous, knowing she would get no enjoyment out of it. She sat on the edge of the bed and slowly slid under the covers.

As soon as his hand touched her leg, she said the one thing she thought would turn him off.

"Sincere, I'm pregnant."

He stopped in his tracks, a deer-caught-in-head-lights look on his face. She braced herself for what was next. Quietly, he got out of the bed and walked out of the room, slamming the bedroom door behind him. She exhaled as she turned on her side, closing her eyes, and soon fell asleep.

Chapter Ten

Missing in Action
1987

"Where the hell is Sincere?" Brooklyn yelled. She was in unbearable pain as she prepared to bring her daughter into the world. Sincere was missing in action, and she was furious.

Wanda stood by her side, holding a warm cloth over Brooklyn's head, as the nurse came in every few minutes and checked on her. Wanda had recently come back into Brooklyn's life and was now her only friend. She looked at her watch. She'd called Sincere over an hour ago, and he'd promised to be there in fifteen minutes. She looked down at Brooklyn and the distress she was in and felt her pain.

"I'm gonna go try him again, OK," Wanda said as Brooklyn cried out in pain.

The unit was pretty quiet as Wanda quickly walked down the hall toward the waiting room, where the pay phone was located. She was annoyed but tried to keep her cool as she dialed his pager number and put in the call-back number. She waited patiently for the next five minutes until he called back.

"Hello," Wanda said.

"Dis Sincere. Who dis?"

"It's Wanda. Where are you?" she said, annoyed by his calmness. Brooklyn was pushing out his baby, and he was acting like he didn't have a care in the world.

"I'm on my way. Did she have the baby?"

"No, Sincere! You said that over an hour ago. She needs you."

"I said I'm on my way. The longer I sit and talk to you, the longer it'll take me to get up there. Just tell her I'll be there in ten minutes." He hung up the phone.

Wanda looked at the receiver and shook her head. She hung the phone up and headed back down the hall toward Brooklyn's room. She could hear her screams getting louder as she got closer to the door.

Sincere sat on the edge of his bed, his face buried in his hands. He was in no rush to get up to the hospital, but he knew he'd never hear the end of it if he didn't make it up there. He looked over his shoulder at the young female laying beside him. He got up from the bed and grabbed his pants from the floor. The loose change in his pockets jingled, waking up his female companion.

"Where are you going?" Stacey asked as she focused on him.

"To the hospital. Brooklyn is in labor. I'm going to leave you some cab money."

"Cab money?" She sat up. "Why can't you take me home?"

"Didn't you just hear what I said? I need to get to the hospital. I'm already late. I don't need no detours and shit!" he yelled as he buttoned his shirt. He grabbed his wallet off the nightstand, pulled out a hundred dollars, and threw it on the bed.

Stacey sat there pouting. As much as she didn't want to believe it, she knew she'd never mean as much to him as Brooklyn did. She'd spent most of her teenage years trying to keep up with Brooklyn, and though some would agree that they were equally beautiful, it was just something about Brooklyn that always made her the center of attention.

She looked at the money lying on the bed as Sincere walked out of the door. She could've cared less about Brooklyn or her baby. They hadn't been friends in over a year, and she liked it better that way. No longer did she have to live in her shadow. She'd always had a crush on Sincere, even before Brooklyn was attracted to him. It just so happened that Brooklyn, as outgoing as she was, managed to snag him first.

Sincere sped through the streets and made it to the hospital about twenty minutes later. After finding his way to the delivery room, he took a deep breath before going inside. He knew Brooklyn would be pissed that he took so long to arrive.

As soon as he entered the room, both Brooklyn and Wanda gave him the evil eye. Wanda brushed past him to head out to the waiting room, rolling her eyes as she did.

Within minutes of his arrival, Brooklyn gave birth to their daughter Sasha. Sincere attempted to play father of the year, but Brooklyn wasn't the least bit impressed.

After she'd recovered, she was taken over to the room she would occupy for the next two days. She couldn't wait to be alone with Sincere, to give him a piece of her mind.

After the nurse gave Brooklyn a lunch tray and headed out of the room, she tore into him. "So where were you?" she asked, staring at him almost as if she could see through him.

"Taking care of some business." He calmly sat down in the chair across the room.

Brooklyn could feel her blood boiling. "Which bitch was it this time, Sincere?"

"This is not the time or the place for this shit, Brooklyn. Can we talk about this another time?"

"No, we can't. You know, every time I think that things are getting better between us, you go and do some shit. I know you like the back of my hand, Sincere, and I know you were with somebody today. I'm giving birth to your child and you couldn't even be here for me."

Sincere sat there silent. He wasn't really in the mood for an argument and figured she'd drop it if he didn't feed into it. Besides, regardless of his answer, he realized she'd already had her mind set.

"Just be honest for once in your life. Just tell me who it was."

He was trying to avoid hurting her any more. The fact that she was still probing him for more information showed that she was fed up. Prior to Stacey, he'd never really dealt with a female on the side who stood a chance of ruining their relationship, but he was positive, if he told her the truth, things would be over. Trying to force her to stay wouldn't work at this point. He took a deep breath, as he looked over in her direction.

Brooklyn sat there waiting for a response. She wanted to know the truth. That would give her the boost she needed to walk away from him.

"It was Stacey. Are you happy now?"

Chapter Eleven

Fool in Love
1987

"Mom, I have a show. Please just keep the baby here."

"I'm not going to be a fucking live-in babysitter," Janice yelled from the kitchen of their small row home. "You should've stayed with that nigga so he could take care of you. Then you wouldn't have to work."

After breaking up with Sincere, Brooklyn tried to focus on her career, but lugging a baby everywhere was more difficult than she expected. School was out of the question as well, since there wasn't enough time to balance it all in one day. Sincere refused to help her financially unless she decided to give their relationship another chance.

"Mom, I'm not going to argue. I have to go." She grabbed her coat and walked out of the door. She walked to the corner to catch the bus to the agency, hoping she wouldn't be late. She was warned after she had the baby about missing events and the possibility of being dropped from her contract.

She heard the loud thumping of music and spotted Sincere's car coming around the corner. She was hoping he didn't stop.

He noticed her standing on the corner and slowed down in front of her. His passenger seat was occupied by a female, so he got out of the car instead of rolling down the window.

"Hey, you need a ride?" he asked as he leaned on the hood of his car.

"No. Buses are running," she spat. Brooklyn was still pissed about the way he'd been acting, as if she'd done something to him, when in reality, he'd treated her like shit all along.

"Why the attitude, Brook? I'm trying to be a gentleman here."

"What the fuck do you know about being a gentleman? How about you learn to be a father, unless you forgot you have a daughter."

"Come on, Brooklyn, I told you the deal. I'm not trying to argue with you. It's cold as shit outside, and I was just trying to be nice and drop you off, but if you want to be a bitch about it, fine."

"Whatever, Sincere. How are you going to offer me a ride, with a bitch in the car, anyway?"

"Because I don't care about her. I love you. I'd put her ass out on this bus stop for you."

Brooklyn stood there with her lips twisted. She believed every word of what he said, but she knew behind the act of kindness was something sinister.

"All right. Well, don't ever say I didn't offer," he said before walking toward the driver's side door to get in.

She thought about the time, and how cold it was. "Wait. I'll get in," she said.

He smiled and shook his head. He instructed the female to get in the backseat, to allow Brooklyn to sit in the front.

Brooklyn felt extremely uncomfortable with the situation, but she was focused on getting to the agency on time and tried to ignore it.

"So where do you need to go?"

"To the agency."

"You're back at that now, huh. Well, that's good. I guess you gotta get paid somehow, right?" he said, trying to be ironic. The way he figured, she would have to come back to him eventually, once she ran out of money.

"Yeah, especially since you don't pay any child support," she shot back.

Sincere laughed. He loved pissing her off.

The female in the backseat sat shaking her head at the two of them bickering like a married couple. She knew all about Brooklyn since she was all Sincere talked about. Everything she did was compared to her.

They continued to go back and forth the entire fifteen-minute ride. Pulling up in front of the agency, she quickly unlocked the door and got out without a good-bye.

Smiling, he watched her walk inside. He definitely missed having her around and planned on getting her back.

Brooklyn ran up the stairs and made it there in the nick of time. Mesa was sitting at her desk waiting on her to arrive.

"I was just about to call you. Glad you made it on time."

"I told you I'd be here," she replied out of breath.

"Well, you can go sit and wait up front. The van will be here in a few to drive you over to the site."

"OK."

The show was perfect, making Brooklyn feel like she was back on top.

Once they returned to the agency, she was shocked to find Sincere waiting outside in his car. *What the hell?* she thought.

He got out of the car as soon as she stepped out of the van.

"What are you doing here?"

"I'm trying to make sure you make it home safe, that's all."

"If I didn't know any better, I'd think you were stalking me."

He laughed. "I'm not stalking you. I care about you whether you believe it or not. Look, I'm being nice here, Brooklyn. Give me a break."

"Where's the chick that was with you earlier? Better yet, where's Stacey?"

"Who cares? Why does everything have to be an argument? I don't care about either one of them. If I did, I wouldn't have sat out here for the last hour waiting for you, OK."

As much as Brooklyn wanted to resist him, she couldn't. She still loved him, as much as she tried to deny it. From the outside she'd most likely look like the biggest fool on the planet for going back to him, but there was just something about him that had a hold on her. She smiled inside but tried to keep a straight face as she walked over to the car. She was exhausted with resisting him.

As she sat in the car, Sincere was looking over at her every few seconds, all sorts of nasty thoughts running through his head. Instead of taking her home, he detoured to his house.

Brooklyn already knew what he was planning. Coincidentally, she was thinking the same thing.

Chapter Twelve

One for the Road
1988

Things between Brooklyn and Sincere had been much better. They rarely argued, and for a long time he hadn't placed a hand on her. He'd recently taught her how to drive and purchased her a car. She was now able to get around and make it to appointments on time.

Modeling was also great for her. She had a lunch meeting with a local designer to go over some of his ideas for a spread she was doing for a New York magazine. As she sat at the table waiting for Mark Watts, the designer, she noticed a man sitting across the room at a small table, reading a newspaper and drinking a cappuccino. She had never been so amazed by a man before that day, but something about him was consuming all of her attention. She didn't want to be rude with a continuous stare, so she would take her eyes off him every few seconds to avoid making eye contact.

You could tell by the way that she sat at the table with her legs crossed that she was confident. Her makeup was flawless, and her eyelash extensions made her eyes pop. Her jet-black hair hung beneath her shoulders, and every time she turned her head it bounced.

She almost dropped her glass when he noticed her stare and smiled. The light and warmth from the gesture had her heart racing. She tried to ignore the fact that he was now returning the stares. *Damn!* she thought to herself. *How did I manage to be so obvious?*

She retrieved a book from her purse and acted as if she was reading it. She could feel his eyes burning a hole in the side of her face. She was saved by the bell when Mark walked in.

"Sorry I'm late," he said as he took off his jacket and hung it over the back of the chair. "Traffic was rough today."

"Oh, no problem. I was a little late myself," she lied, focusing all of her attention on him. "So what do you have for me? I don't doubt that it's anything less than extraordinary." She smiled.

"I'm glad you have so much confidence in me," he said as he pulled his portfolio from his briefcase.

She was so excited about Mark's designs, she'd completely forgotten about the game she was playing with the handsome stranger.

Mark agreed to have the samples ready by the end of the week, and they shook hands before he rose from the table and walked away.

She glanced across the room, where the stranger had been sitting, and noticed that the table was now occupied by a group of teenagers. She flagged down the waitress to get the check and was surprised to find out that the bill had already been paid.

"By whom?" she asked.

"The man who was sitting at the table across the way," she said, pointing in the direction of the teenagers. "He left his card and told me to give it to you."

Brooklyn was smiling from ear to ear as she silently read the name. She wasn't sure how she would contact him, with Sincere always around.

She drove over to Sincere's house and found it empty. She decided to get dinner started and arouse him at the same time. So she cooked naked, hoping he would come home alone.

Sincere was just finishing his runs for the night and was on his way home. He planned to run back out later that night, but he knew if he didn't spend time with Brooklyn, it would turn into a screaming match. As he opened the door he could smell the aroma of chicken and garlic. *She must have read my mind,* he thought, *because I'm starving.*

He entered the kitchen and spotted her naked body, which turned him on immediately. He forgot about how hungry he was. He walked over to her and palmed her soft cheeks. He softly kissed her on the neck as she tilted her head to the side to give him full access.

She moaned slightly to welcome him, and as she was practically dripping wet from the excitement, he slowly eased down to his knees and began to playfully place bites across her behind. She loved it and continued to moan as she bent over the sink to push her ass out a little farther.

Sincere pushed her right leg up, so she could place her knee on the counter. Her wetness now staring him in the face, his tongue was ready to taste her juices. He stiffened his tongue as he moved closer and slowly licked her mound from front to back. "Ummm!" he moaned, enjoying the wonderful taste. As her fresh scent tickled his nose, he went to work with his tongue, causing her to tremble.

Brooklyn grabbed a hold of the faucet as she had one orgasm after another.

He paused. "You like this shit, baby?"

"I love it, baby. Now keep going."

He moved up to her asshole as he stuck two fingers inside of her tunnel. She moved back and forth on his finger as he used his tongue to make love to her from behind. She was trying to grab hold of anything, to keep her composure. He sped up the pace, making the experience even more electrifying.

As she continued to release her juices, he took it all in. After draining her of all of her energy, he pulled his finger from inside of her and slowly sucked the remaining juices from them.

"I'm starving, baby. I could eat a whole horse," he said as he stood up from the ground.

They both burst into laughter.

"You are so crazy," she said as she eased her leg off the counter.

"That's why you love me." Smiling, he eased in to kiss her lips. Then he headed to the bathroom to wash his face.

Stacey crossed his mind as he looked into the mirror and tried to figure out how he would get away from Brooklyn to give her a call. He hurried through the meal that Brooklyn had prepared and broke the news to her that he had to run out to take care of some business. She, of course, was pissed, but after he promised her a round two of what she had earlier, she quickly let the anger go.

Within minutes he was on his way to his brother's house to get a quick shower and call Stacey. He'd been thinking about her a lot lately. As much as he cared about Brooklyn, Stacey had also become special to him during their breakup. He stopped at a pay phone and dialed her number.

After the second ring, the tone of her beautiful voice boomed through the receiver. "Hello."

"Hey, Stacey. It's Sin."

"What's up, stranger? Haven't seen or heard from you in a while."

"I missed you, and I wanted to take you out to dinner so we could talk. That is if you don't have any plans tonight."

"No, I don't have any plans." Stacey smiled. She had missed him too but figured, if she gave him some space, he'd come back to her. "Dinner isn't a problem. Just let me know the place and time, and I'll be there," she said, trying not to sound overly excited, because the truth was, she was damn near ready to jump through the roof.

He definitely didn't expect the conversation to go the way it did but was glad he'd decided to call. They set a time to meet, and he headed to Sidney's house, where he always kept a spare outfit.

He knocked instead of using his key, since this was a surprise visit. He didn't want to risk walking in on Sidney ass naked with a woman, which had happened plenty times in the past.

"Hey. What's up, Sin?" Sidney said, smiling as he opened the door. He reached in to give him dap.

"I just need to use your shower and change real quick."

"What? You and that chick are fighting again? I told you to leave her ass alone a long time ago," he said, moving into the house.

"No. Actually, I have a date, and I can't go back home to change."

"Hell yeah, you can change. It's about time you came to your senses. Who's the lucky lady?"

"It's Stacey."

"Aww, man, I thought it was somebody new. How the hell you gonna cheat on Brooklyn with her again?"

"Man, I love Brooklyn, don't get me wrong, but I feel like the relationship is forced. She doesn't really want to be with me."

"But why Stacey? Damn, that was her best friend."

"Shit, they haven't been friends for a long time, and the truth is, they probably will never be friends. I'm really trying to get to know Stacey to see what can happen."

"Well, if you want my opinion, I'd just leave both of them alone. You can have pretty much any chick you want. Why backtrack?"

"Man, I'm going to take a shower. We'll talk about it later."

"All right. Well, don't come running to me when one of those chicks cut your ass up." Sidney laughed.

Sincere quickly got changed and headed down Center City to meet with Stacey. He was almost knocked off his feet when he walked into the restaurant and saw her. Her hair was pulled into a ponytail that hung over her shoulder, and she was wearing a black strapless dress that stopped just above her knee, her black pumps with the bow on top complementing the dress perfectly.

Stacey smiled as he headed over to the table and stood up just as he got close. She held out her arms to meet him with a hug.

"You look amazing," he said, getting a whiff of her perfume.

"Thanks. You look sexy as always." She smiled, and they sat down at the table.

Sincere was excited. He was losing interest in his relationship with Brooklyn and was hoping to get something started with her.

"So what's going on with you and Brooklyn?" She took a sip of her water. "You dropped me like a hot cake when she came back into your life."

He hesitated for a second, caught off guard by the question. He wasn't even positive that she knew about him getting back with her. "Wow! I wasn't expecting that."

She laughed. "Well, you brought me here to talk, right? I'm just curious, because you never asked me on a date before. So what's up? I'm used to going straight to your house, getting screwed, and being dropped off with a few dollars in my pocket."

"Damn! I was that bad?" he asked, realizing how he treated women.

"Yeah, you were."

"Well, that's the old me, OK. I asked you here so I could apologize. To be honest, I'm not sure why I wanted Brooklyn back. I guess it's just the history, and we have a child together. You know what I mean?"

"So what's different now? You're still with her?"

"I realize that what we had is over. But I'm a man; I can't be alone. But if you want to make this work, I will let her go."

"Are you bullshitting me, Sincere, or are you serious?"

"I'm serious."

"Well, make it happen," she said, smiling from ear to ear. For once, she felt confident that she was winning the race and no longer had to try and keep up with Brooklyn. The rest of the dinner was perfect, ending with his promise to be with her.

Sincere went home, knowing that Brooklyn would be pissed and probably start a fight, which was just what he needed to end it all.

Chapter Thirteen

Meeting in the Ladies' Room
1988

"I need a place to stay. Is there any way you can help me?" Brooklyn whispered to Mesa from the small bedroom at her mother's house.

"What's wrong?"

"I just got in a huge fight with my mom, Sincere and I broke up, and I really have nowhere else to go."

"I can come get you, Brooklyn, but the boarding house doesn't allow babies."

"That's fine. She's OK with my mom. She won't hurt her. I just have to get away."

"OK. Where are you now? I'll come and get you."

"I'm across the street from my mom's, at Ms. Rose's house."

"OK. Give me an hour or so, and I'll be there."

"OK." Brooklyn hung up and patiently waited for Mesa to arrive.

Brooklyn's fight with her mother had gotten totally out of control. What started off as a verbal spat quickly turned physical, scaring the kids. Lately, Brooklyn's temper had been hard to manage, and combined with her mother's lack of parenting, it was bound to happen eventually. She felt like her career was going to slip away if she didn't get focused, that the longer she stayed in that house unhappy, the more likely it would be to happen.

Once Mesa arrived, Brooklyn happily ran out of the house to meet her. She was excited about the possibilities of being out on her own. Mesa explained that she'd be sharing a room with another model, that the agency would take an additional percentage from her checks as payment for room and board, and Brooklyn easily agreed, knowing it was for the best.

Just as she was putting her bags into the trunk, Sincere pulled up behind the car. It was just like him to show up at the worst times. Surely, she wasn't in the mood to talk, fuss, or fight with him.

"Where are you going?"

"That's none of your concern, Sincere. Sasha is in the house. I'm not your child."

"Yes, it is my concern. Your brother called and said you and your mom were fighting. What happened?"

"Look, Sincere, I have to go. I really don't have time to stand here and hash out my family problems with you. If you were so fucking concerned for me, you wouldn't have left me for that tramp of yours. My life is no longer your business." Brooklyn closed the trunk and began to walk over toward the passenger side door.

Sincere grabbed hold of her arm. "You realize you'll always be mine. I don't give a fuck how far you go to try and hide."

She looked down at his hand and then back up to his face. "Let go of me," she responded, through clenched teeth.

Mesa got out of the car when she noticed him holding her arm. "Let her go, or I'll call the cops."

He laughed as he slowly let go of her arm. "I'll let go for now, but remember what I said." He backed away and headed back to his car, which was still running. He quickly sped off, leaving Brooklyn and Mesa standing there.

"Are you OK?" Mesa asked, placing her hand on Brooklyn's shoulder.

"Yes, I'm fine. Can we just go?"

Brooklyn was even more confident at that very moment that she was making the right decision to get away, even if just for a little while.

With so much on her mind, the ride to the boarding house seemed especially long, and she was more than relieved when they made it there. When she went up to her room, a female, introduced as Natasha, was sprawled out across the bed.

"Well, I'll leave you two to get acquainted. Brooklyn, I'll call you tomorrow, OK," Mesa said, walking out of the room.

Natasha looked over at Brooklyn, taking a glance at her clothing. She didn't appear too impressed by the young beautiful female, who appeared to lack the confidence needed to make it in the business. Natasha knew, coming in, that she had to find a way to outshine the other females in the industry.

Brooklyn, though exhausted, immediately noticed that Natasha didn't look too fond of her.

"So what's your story?" Natasha finally spoke as she sat up on the edge of the bed.

"What do you mean?"

"I mean, what brings you here? Everyone here is running away from something, so what's your story?"

"I'm not running from anything. I just wanted to try being on my own."

"Yeah, I guess if you say that enough, you'll believe it, but I'm sure it's bullshit."

Brooklyn was shocked by her abruptness and wasn't quite sure how to respond. Afraid it would lead to a confrontation, she tried to brush it off, but Natasha wasn't through yet.

"You look like the type that has man trouble. Am I right?"

"No, you're not, and I'd appreciate it if you just—"

"Girl, I'm just playing with you. I love fooling with the new kid on the block. I am definitely not trying to be all up in your business." Natasha laughed.

Brooklyn wasn't laughing immediately but eventually let out a giggle. She hadn't laughed in a long time about anything, so it was sort of like therapy.

Following her first night at the house, she and Natasha spent a lot of their time together. She loved all of the knowledge she got from hanging around someone who'd been modeling for a while. She would call home daily and would stop in to see Sasha and her brothers on the weekend.

Most wouldn't understand how she could leave her daughter behind, but she felt like she had no choice if she was ever going to make it big. Some day she was certain that her daughter would understand why she made most of the choices she did, including steering clear of her father.

Eventually, she picked up a lot of Natasha's habits as well, including the use of cocaine. The first time she saw her snorting the powder through a straw, she didn't know what to think. Natasha quickly explained that it was necessary, to stay thin and keep the energy she needed to do all of the events and shoots. She coaxed Brooklyn into trying it out, and Brooklyn was hooked from that day on.

Mesa noticed a change in Brooklyn and pulled her aside at one event.

"Hey, I just wanted to talk to you because I've noticed you and Natasha getting pretty close."

"Yeah, that's my girl. I'm glad you put me in the room with her because most of the other girls in the house are complete duds." She laughed.

"Well, that's not what I mean. I'm aware of her habits, and I don't want to see you screw up your future, following behind her, if you know what I mean."

"Not really. I think she's great. I get a lot of good information from her, and she actually keeps me focused. Being away from my family all the time was hard, so it's nice to have someone close to talk to when I'm confused and things get rough."

"I need you to be careful. I was your age once, and I know how temptation can get the best of you. I just would hate to see you fail. When I saw you at your school, I saw something special. I just want you to succeed."

"You don't have to worry about me. I'm going to make you proud. You believed in me even after I got pregnant, and I appreciate that."

"Just don't let me down. I have a lot riding on you, and it could be bad for the both of us if things don't work out. Just don't be so easily influenced. What's good for the goose is not good for the gander, OK. Keep that in mind."

"I will."

Mesa reached in to hug her before letting her return to hair and makeup. Brooklyn knew exactly what she was referring to, but she was confident that she could handle her own. She could appreciate her concern, though she wasn't worried in the least bit. The decision to trust Natasha was one that she felt was the better of any that she'd made in the past.

Mesa watched as Brooklyn pranced around, high strung. She was hoping that she could be strong enough to walk away from it all, just as she had walked away from Sincere.

Chapter Fourteen

Catching Up
1989

"Hey, girl. I missed you!" Wanda yelled as she hugged Brooklyn. The two had met at a Center City restaurant to catch up on the gossip.

"I know we have so much to talk about. Have you seen Stacey?"

"Not lately, but I heard she's pregnant."

"Wow! Really? I never thought I'd see the day she'd betray me the way she did. I was sure, when we were younger, that we'd be friends forever. Obviously I was sadly mistaken."

"Well, you know she was always trying to compete with you. I think she always felt like she was living in your shadows and would do practically anything to get in the limelight."

"Well, I don't care how hard she tries, she'll never be me, honey!" Brooklyn laughed. "I'm sure he's whupping her ass, so hey, all I can do is say thanks."

"You think so?"

"I know so, girl. There is no way he'll change for her. Hell, I'm prime meat, girl, and he wouldn't change for me. I don't even know why I was mad that she took him away at first."

Wanda laughed. "You are crazy, girl."

"I'm serious. I couldn't be happier now. Things are looking up for me. I mean, I miss having a man around every now and then, but you know it is what it is. I'm so busy, I barely have time to sleep."

"Well, I'm really happy for you. I only want the best for you."

"That's why we're friends." Brooklyn smiled.

Brooklyn refused to show how much it really bothered her that Stacey was pregnant. She'd truly just gotten over her relationship with Sincere. It wasn't just that she cared about him, but now her daughter would be forced to share. She could never imagine sleeping with someone who was in a relationship with any of her friends, but Stacey was cut from a different cloth.

"Well, enough about her, girl. Let's order."

When the two finished their meal, they went to the mall to do some shopping. Catching up with Wanda was much needed.

After two hours of walking the mall, they were headed out when they spotted Stacey and her group of friends in their path to the door. The two hadn't come face to face in almost a year.

Wanda was nervous, hoping the meeting wouldn't turn into an all-out brawl.

The two stood face to face and locked eyes. As the staring match continued, you could feel the heat rising from both of them. The hatred for Brooklyn was never clear. From the outside looking in, you'd know that she did everything in her power to keep Stacey afloat, so it came out of left field when Stacey became such a backstabber.

Wanda tried to keep her eyes on the both of them, expecting someone to snap.

"Well, well, well . . . if it isn't Ms. Brooklyn."

"Sure is. In the flesh. See me and weep."

"Please. No need. There's nothing special about it, from what I see."

"Yeah? Well, your man surely thinks so."

"I highly doubt that. He's so over you."

"Yeah, I see he has you fooled. I bet he's beating your ass too."

Taken aback, Stacey fumbled for a reply. "You're real funny, Brooklyn, but try again. See, I'm not you. I guess that shows how much more he cares about me."

"Look, I'd love to stand here and continue this useless chat with you, but we both know the truth, and bickering about it won't change anything." Brooklyn grabbed Wanda by the hand and brushed past Stacey, who stood shaking her head, and they headed out of the mall.

"I'm so proud of you. I thought for sure you were going to deck her."

"She's so not worth it. Besides, I'm not trying to go to jail for hitting a pregnant woman. I could see her ass now pressing charges on me and having my ass in handcuffs."

"Well, drive safe. I'm so glad we got to hang out. Don't make it so long the next time." Wanda reached in to hug Brooklyn.

"I won't, I promise."

As the two parted ways, both smiling, Brooklyn was proud of herself. Every inch of her wanted to lay Stacey out cold, but she knew it wasn't the right thing to do. That she was over Sincere made it that much more simple. She was tired of being angry and was ready to start living. Now that she'd seen Stacey, she felt better about moving forward without either of them on her mind.

Chapter Fifteen

Second Chances
1990

Brooklyn was glowing as she made her way around the room in a tight-fitting black mini dress and red pumps. The party, a housewarming and contract celebration for Natasha, was packed, so most of the attendees were models and industry professionals. She graced the room with a half-empty glass, dancing and floating off the cocaine she'd snorted a half-hour earlier. She spotted a familiar face off to the side of the room and quickly grabbed a hold of her friend to confirm.

"Who's the cutie over in the corner?"

"What cutie?" Natasha asked, quickly doing a surveillance of the room.

"The dark-skinned over by the bar."

"Oh, that's Jay. He's an architect."

"I thought that was him. I met him a while back. Well, we didn't officially meet, but he slipped me his card and paid a tab at a restaurant. I never called because I lost the card, but I could never forget his fine ass."

"Well, go talk to him, girl. I have to do some more mingling." Natasha nudged Brooklyn in his direction.

Brooklyn fixed her dress and ran her fingers through her hair as she walked over to where the guy was sitting. He looked up as soon as he noticed her standing near him.

"Hi, Jay, I'm Brooklyn. Do you remember me?"

"How could I forget your face?" He quickly looked her up and down.

"Good. I'm glad I ran into you. I lost your card, so I never had the chance to formally thank you for paying my tab."

"No problem. Obviously you were meant to see me again."

"Well, I'm glad I did."

"So you're a model, huh?"

"Yeah. Can't you tell?" She playfully rubbed her hands down across her hips.

He laughed. "Definitely. And I like what I see." He paused and licked his lips. "I was just going to get out of here. Do you want to come with me?"

"Where are you going?"

"I was going home, but I can leave you my number again, if you don't want to go."

"I didn't say that. I was just checking. Let me tell Natasha that I'm leaving, and I'll meet you at the door."

"OK, cool."

After talking to Natasha, Brooklyn headed to the door, where she met Jay. Brooklyn knew the night would probably end with sex, and was hoping it wouldn't be the last time. She hadn't been with a man since Sincere and was definitely yearning for some satisfaction. Tall, dark-skinned, and successful, Jay was everything she wanted in a man. It was also a plus that he wasn't a drug dealer.

They got into his car and were on their way.

"I'm going to make a stop first. I want to show you something."

"OK," she said nervously. She wasn't sure what was coming next but decided to go with the flow.

They pulled up in front of a restaurant, which was totally dark. She was confused. "What are we doing here?"

"This is a restaurant I designed. It's almost complete. I just wanted to take you inside so you could see my work."

They got out of the car and entered the building. Jay flicked on the lights. Brooklyn was amazed by the décor. She turned around to compliment him and was met by his face. She took a deep breath as he put his lips to hers. She instantly felt her body temperature rise. He put his hands on the side of her face to intensify the kiss, and she got chills up and down her spine. He was taking control, and it was turning her on.

As his tongue massaged hers, he used both hands to reach around and unzip her dress, and it fell to the floor. He released his grip and slowly pushed her back to the chair placed at one of the small round tables. He sat down and watched as she turned around and bent over to remove her shoes, her ass pointed in his direction. He reached out to grab it, and she quickly moved away.

"Not yet, no touching," she said playfully.

Jay smiled as he sat back in the chair and continued watching her. She backed up a little farther and headed to the stereo system. The music began to play, and her body began to move to the notes. It took everything in him not to jump up and tackle her. He wanted to feel her and taste her, but he held it together long enough to enjoy the show.

She slowly unhooked her bra and released one breast at a time. Her perfect nipples at attention, she used two fingers to massage them, moving her hips in a slow wind. Each time she moved her hips to the front and down to the floor, the lips of her pussy showed from the sides of her panties.

Brooklyn was killing him, and she knew it. She turned around and slowly slid her panties over her round ass. Then she stepped out of them and threw them over her shoulder, so he could catch them.

Jay picked them up off his lap and put them to his nose. He inhaled the sweet scent of her juices and became even more anxious to taste her.

By this time she was on her knees and bent over on top of one of the tables. She spread her legs and stuck two fingers inside of her tunnel. He stared as she moved them in and out. As the juices began to flow, she picked up the pace. She moaned as she reached an orgasm.

Jay could feel his dick getting hard. He stuck his hand into his pants and began to massage it. He kept his eyes open, not wanting to miss anything.

She turned around and spread her legs wide. While slowly massaging her clit with one hand, she used her free hand to motion him to come closer. "Come on, taste these juices," she said in a seductive tone. "I want to fill you up."

Jay wasted no time moving over to the table. He got on his knees and licked his lips while staring at her pussy. He slowly stuck out his tongue and licked her from top to bottom. Brooklyn moaned immediately as he began to make circles on her clit. The juices soon began to pour out of her, and he sucked them up, not releasing a drop. He pushed her legs up higher and stuck his tongue deep into her tunnel.

"Right there! Yes!" she said aloud.

Soon she was reaching another orgasm and screaming with delight. "Come on, baby, let me satisfy you," she said as he stood up from the ground.

Jay quickly dropped his pants and stepped out of them. Then he slid off his underwear.

Brooklyn instructed him to sit down. Her pussy dripping wet, she climbed on top of him and began to move up and down with force. As her ass hit his legs, you could hear the slapping sound echoing in the room.

And the two continued the sexual escapade until he couldn't hold on to the juices that began to flow freely from him. Afterward, both of them were satisfied with the night and looked forward to many more like it.

Chapter Sixteen

Love in the Air
1990

Following their first night together Brooklyn and Jay were inseparable. Rarely would you see one without the other. He'd even picked up the slack with Sasha, where Sincere fell short.

Brooklyn was able to hide her drug habit from him, though she was almost caught a few times. She was so used to the energy she got from cocaine, she normally didn't go a day without it.

Sincere was still involved with Stacey, and Brooklyn was actually glad, since he no longer had her to focus on. For the most part, things were perfect, but there was always that calm before the storm.

Hanging out with Wanda had slowly faded, as she and Natasha became closer. She felt bad, since Wanda had walked away from her group of friends for her. They were moving in two different directions, and that put a major strain on their friendship.

Four months into her relationship with Jay, they had their first big fight. For Brooklyn, it came out of left field, since he was a pretty easygoing guy. She was on her way over to his house, where he sat patiently waiting for her arrival.

"Hey, baby." She walked over to the chair he was sitting in to greet him with a kiss.

"What the fuck is this?" he yelled. He turned his face and raised his hand, showing the small plastic bag filled with white powder that he'd stumbled across.

"I don't know, Jay. Where did you find that?"

"You don't know? Do I look like a total asshole to you, Brooklyn?" he yelled. "You know exactly where I found it, and stop trying to play dumb, because it's not working."

Brooklyn was now walking away from him and pacing the floor, trying to figure out what to say next. She knew that the day would come when she'd have to be honest about her addiction, but she wasn't expecting it to come quite yet. Her mind racing, it was almost as if she'd stepped out of the situation completely, as she could no longer hear what he was saying.

Jay stood there yelling, waiting for a response, knowing full well what the contents of the package were.

"Look, I was holding it for someone else," she finally responded.

"You're just gonna keep the lies coming, right?" He walked over to her and, before she knew it, hit her across the face with the back of his hand, knocking her to the ground.

Instantly her mind flashed back to the days of her tumultuous relationship with Sincere. She knew from past experiences not to move or attempt to get away, since that would only fuel his anger.

"Get your ass up!" he yelled.

If there was one thing that disgusted Jay, it was a liar. After all, it was right in front of his face, and she still couldn't be honest. All of the trust that he once had quickly drained away at that moment.

"Now are you going to be honest?" he asked, his hand gripping the collar of her shirt.

Tears pouring out of her eyes, she prayed that he wouldn't hit her again. She hesitated to respond, afraid that whatever she said would be the wrong thing.

His teeth clenched, his eyes practically bulging out of their sockets, he balled his fist, preparing to strike her once more.

She yelled, "OK, OK, it's mine! I'm sorry, Jay. I didn't want you to find out. I didn't want anyone to find out about it. Please don't hit me again. I have a photo shoot tomorrow."

Jay punched her, causing her to fall yet again. This time she could feel her nose running. He stood over her, yelling obscenities, as she placed her hand under her nose, trying to stop the blood from hitting the floor.

"I can't believe I'm dealing with a fucking drug addict! Does this shit mean that much to you, huh? What if Sasha got a hold of this? Do you even use your head?" He opened the plastic bag and poured the powder over her head as she sat sobbing and bracing herself up with one hand.

Brooklyn questioned whether or not she deserved this. She didn't believe anyone could be unlucky enough to have two men beat on her.

"Get yourself cleaned up. If I ever see this shit again, you'll regret it. I promise you that." He grabbed his jacket and walked out of the house.

She got up from the floor with her face throbbing and went into the bathroom to look in the mirror. She grabbed a washcloth and patted her face, all the while blaming herself for what just happened. She knew she wouldn't be in the current situation if she hadn't brought the drugs into the house. Was it enough to leave? She didn't think so. She'd stuck it out with Sincere through worse.

With her hands holding both sides of the sink, she quickly said a prayer.

She went back out and grabbed her purse, which was still lying on the floor in the living room, to retrieve her makeup. With skill she covered her face with foundation and blush to hide the redness.

After she was done, she called Wanda. She hadn't spoken to her in a while and was actually the only person she felt comfortable talking to when things got bad.

"Hello," Wanda said, sounding as if she was asleep.

"Hey, Wanda. It's Brooklyn. Did I wake you?"

"Hey, Brooklyn. No, I'm awake. How have you been? I haven't spoken to you in a while."

"Not good, Wanda, not good at all," she said with a whisper. She was trying to keep her voice down, in the event Jay walked back into the house.

"What's wrong?"

"It's Jay. He just hit me twice, busted my nose and all."

"What?" she yelled. "Where are you?"

"I'm still at his house. It's all my fault, Wanda."

"It's no excuse for that, Brooklyn. When are you going to learn to stop being a punching bag for these men?"

"He found my stash of cocaine and he—"

"Cocaine? What the hell were you doing with that?"

"It was mine. I've been using it for a while. I can barely make it through the day without it. I should have kept it with me. I was stupid to think I could hide it in his house."

"Look, come over my house, so we can talk, OK. You called me for a reason, and I'm here to help you."

"I can't, Wanda. I have to be here when he comes back. But if you don't hear from me by tomorrow, come check on me, OK."

"I don't like the sound of that, Brooklyn."

"Just check on me, OK. I have to go." *Click.*

Brooklyn hung up the phone as soon as she heard Jay's keys in the door. She was truly more afraid than she'd ever been and didn't want to piss him off for any other reason.

Jay showed up with flowers. He felt bad about the earlier incident and wanted to apologize for hitting her. He did love her and never intended to hurt her.

Brooklyn accepted the flowers and acted as if it never happened.

For the remainder of the night, Jay tried to make it up to her in every way possible, knowing he could potentially lose her. At that point, not being with her wasn't an option for him. He was becoming obsessed, believing he couldn't live without her.

Chapter Seventeen

Game Time
1991

"What are you doing here?" Brooklyn said to Sincere, who stood in the doorway.

"I came to check on my family."

"Family? You lost your family the day you slept with that whore."

"That was a mistake, Brooklyn, but that's not why I'm here. I heard through the grapevine your man is beating on you."

"What? Who the hell told you that lie? Not every man is like you, Sincere."

"Look, can I come in so we can talk?"

"Hell no, you can't come in. Sasha isn't here, and Jay would flip if he walked in and saw you here."

"Oh, so you are scared of him?"

"I didn't say that. I just don't feel like arguing with him, that's all."

"Whatever, Brooklyn. I know you like the back of my hand, and I know when something is wrong. I just want to talk, that's all. I'll feel better if I know that everything is OK. My daughter lives here too, you know. I can't have her living in a hostile environment."

"Since when do you care about your daughter? Hell, I thought you forgot that you even had one."

Sincere stepped up and kissed her. He didn't speak. He only smiled and licked his sexy lips. Brooklyn couldn't resist. She moved closer to him and kissed him again. Before she knew it, his hands were moving down to the small of her back, and she couldn't stop him. Her pussy was practically dripping wet, and she could feel his bulge growing by the second.

She allowed him to ease off her shorts, while she stood as still as a statue. Her heart was beating so fast, she almost thought she was having a heart attack. He got down, pulling her shorts off, and as she raised her left leg to step out of the shorts, he met her throbbing pussy with his thick lips.

Her knees buckling, she managed to grab a hold of the door handle to keep herself from falling. She leaned back and held on with one hand, while she palmed his head with the other hand to guide him to the spot she needed him to lick. She was moaning so loudly, she was sure people in the other houses could hear through the thin walls. Hell, she would have probably had her ear up to the wall listening and playing with herself.

As she tried to rock her hips, he surprised her yet again, picking her up and resting her thighs on his strong shoulders. His face was buried in her pussy, while she now held on to the wall with both hands and pushed harder against his tongue. She had never had someone who could lick her this good. He was sending her down the slippery slope right into ecstasy. If she could stay in that position forever, she would.

After they had sex and he left, she began to feel guilty about what had just occurred. Somehow she felt that something bad was going to come out of it, but just what, she hadn't figured out yet.

Chapter Eighteen

Is It Me?
1991

Two months following the slipup with Sincere, Brooklyn learned that she was pregnant. Not knowing for certain whether it was Jay's or Sincere's was racking her nerves, to say the least. She'd gone over the dates a million times, just to be sure, in addition to which, she was fighting her cocaine addiction. She didn't remember her pregnancy with Sasha being so hard, but after this she was hoping that she'd never have to experience it again.

The months flew, and as she neared her due date, she became more afraid of the possibility of the unthinkable. She prayed that one mistake wouldn't be the end of it all.

She got dressed and was on her way out of the door when her water broke. Fluid was running down her legs like she'd just peed on herself. She didn't know what to do because she was home alone. She was so afraid, not wanting anything to happen to the baby or herself for that matter. She called Wanda and told her she had to come and get her.

In a flash Wanda came over and drove her to the hospital. When they got to the hospital, she was taken into a labor room immediately, and before she knew it, she was pushing. Jay wasn't there because he was at work, and she didn't have time to call him before the baby arrived.

By the time he got there, it was all over, and their gorgeous baby boy, seven pounds four ounces, was doing fine. Of course they named him Jay Jr. Jay was so happy, she could see it in his eyes.

That night Jay stayed in the hospital with her. He took care of the baby all night. By the time she woke up in the morning, he'd sent him to the nursery.

She turned and looked at him with a smile but instantly noticed that the joyful look from the night before was missing.

"Baby, how come you didn't call me first?"

"Because . . . you were at work, and Wanda was closer."

"But you still should have called me first."

"I was scared, Jay. And why are you so upset?"

"Because I bet Sincere got to see his baby born. That's real fucked up. I wanted to be the first face that my son saw. Instead your girlfriend was."

"So what did you want me do? Stay and have the baby on my own until you got there?"

"You know what, let's forget it."

"You brought it up. Why stop now?"

"I said forget it!" he screamed.

Jay yelled so loud, he startled her. She just sat there shocked, looking at him. He'd acted this way before, but hell, she'd just given birth to his first born. She didn't know why he had to bring Sincere's name up. She just stared at him, and without another word he got up and left.

Brooklyn didn't see him until two days after she got home. He walked in with balloons, a teddy bear, and flowers.

"Hey, baby," he said, smiling. "These are for you."

"Jay, where have you been? Why didn't you call me?"

"I'm sorry. I was just upset and I didn't know how to handle it. I didn't want to hurt you or myself, so I left."

"But I don't understand why you were mad in the first place."

"I don't know either. I'm sorry, baby." He paused, a faraway look in his eyes. Then he quickly said, "Can I hold my son?"

"Of course, you can hold him."

This was the Jay that Brooklyn knew and fell in love with. The warm feeling that he gave her returned. She didn't know what got into him at the hospital and prayed that things would be different.

Jay played with the baby the entire day. Around ten o'clock that night he said he had to go take care of some business and would be back in the morning. Since learning of the pregnancy, he rarely spent the night in the same bed with her, and she didn't understand it. She wanted them to be a real family, but she didn't want to pressure him for fear that she would push him away.

The following day Sincere surprised Brooklyn by bringing the baby a gift.

"Hi, this is for the baby," he said as she opened the door.

"Well, thanks. Do you wanna come in?"

"Yeah, if that's OK, because I wanted to talk."

"Sure, it's fine."

They'd recently started being cordial toward each other. Brooklyn was glad that they could finally act like adults, for the sake of their daughter.

"I know I acted a fool when I found out you were pregnant, but I was upset. I know I did you wrong and that we may never be together again. But I don't want to be enemies. I love you and would rather have you in my life as a friend than not in my life at all."

"So what caused the change?"

"I know I was wrong."

"Well, Sincere, I want to be friends too. I mean, we have a child together, and it's not good for us to be mad at each other all the time. I know I acted funny too, and I apologize. But I think we can be friends, as long as you're serious."

"I am serious." He smiled. "So can I just get a hug?"

"Yeah, you can get a hug." Brooklyn laughed and reached out to hug him.

Right at that moment Jay came in the house. He didn't see them hug, but he heard them talking. He came into the room, his face twisted.

"I'm not interrupting anything, am I?" he said sarcastically.

"No, I was just leaving," Sincere said, getting up to leave. "Thanks for listening, Brooklyn."

"You're welcome."

As soon as Sincere left, Jay started hollering. "What the hell was he doing here?" he said loudly.

"I do have a child by him, you know!"

"Well, she's not here, so he has no business here."

"Well, he needed to talk to me about something."

"Oh, he needed to talk, huh? That's bullshit, Brooklyn. I heard y'all talking."

"And? I didn't do anything wrong."

"Oh, don't try to play innocent with me. I'm not trying to hear that shit. I don't know what kind of asshole you take me for!"

Jay was getting louder by the second. Again, Brooklyn was afraid of him and didn't know what to say or do. She stood there frozen.

"Jay, what has gotten into you?"

"You, that's what! Ever since you found out you were pregnant, you've changed. It's almost like you were guilty of some shit. I mean, everything you say seems like you just made the shit up. I almost feel like I can't trust you anymore."

"No, Jay, you're the one that changed. Where is all of this coming from?" Brooklyn started to cry. "I thought we were doing so good."

"Oh, so now you're going to cry? Keep the tears. I don't have time for this shit. I'm out!" He started walking toward the door.

"Wait!" she said, grabbing his arm.

"Get the hell off of me, Brooklyn! Now!" he screamed in her face.

Brooklyn let him go, and he walked out, slamming the door so hard, the floor shook. She sat in the front room and cried for almost an hour, unsure of what the future held.

Things quickly turned from bad to worse, and Brooklyn often felt like she had no one to turn to. But a chance meeting with Stacey changed it all.

After Stacey finally got the courage to leave Sincere, she and Brooklyn were able to sit down and hash out their differences like women. She apologized to Brooklyn, who accepted her apology. She'd missed her friend and wanted to have her back in her life. The pain she'd caused by her betrayal had worn off, once she was able to get over Sincere herself. She didn't want to be with him. She loved him still but knew he was bad news.

Brooklyn and Stacey began to hang together on a regular basis, since they had a lot of catching up to do. She would soon learn a lot about Stacey and what she used as a crutch when she was down and out.

After a huge blowout with Jay, she turned to her friend.

"Girl, I'm so glad you're home," Brooklyn said as she entered Stacey's row home on Rising Sun Avenue with her two children in tow. It was snowing outside, and she'd caught a cab all the way from North Philly, praying she wouldn't have to turn back around. She'd gotten into a big fight with Jay, one that left her with a black eye, and her children scared of almost every noise they heard on the way over.

Stacey grabbed her under her chin and glanced at her face before shutting the door. "Kids, go ahead in the back room with Janelle." She pointed down the hall, while still looking at Brooklyn's face.

As soon as the kids were out of sight, she began to question her. "What the hell happened to your face?"

"Got into a fight with Jay over money. Does it look real bad?" Her face was throbbing with pain.

"Hell yeah, it looks bad . . . because your eye isn't a damn punching bag. When are you going to leave him, girl? I just don't get it."

"I keep saying that I am, but I don't have shit, Stacey. All of the money has run out, and I have two children to feed. What the hell am I supposed to do? I can't even get a modeling gig to save my life. No one will hire a high school dropout. I'm so lost, I really don't know what to do."

"The same shit you told me to do when Sincere was whupping on my ass—Walk out!" she yelled.

"I wish it was that easy." Brooklyn shook her head as she tried to get comfortable on the sofa. She looked over at her friend, whose face showed pity. "Don't look at me like that."

"I just can't believe what I'm hearing."

"It is what it is, Stacey. I mean, look at me. I'm not the same Brooklyn you used to know." She laughed.

Stacey didn't find humor in what she was saying, though she was absolutely right. The Brooklyn she used to know would have walked away from Jay a long time ago.

"I just need to clear my head, girl. I will be OK," she said, trying to convince herself.

"I have something that might help." Stacey stood up from the chair she was sitting in across from Brooklyn.

"What's that?" Brooklyn asked, hoping it would help take the pain away, whatever it was. She knew her relationship with Jay was far from over, that if she could have just a moment of solace, she'd feel a little bit better.

Stacey led her into her finished basement, to the room in the back behind the washer and dryer. As they neared the room, Brooklyn figured out what she was headed for.

From the outside looking in, you'd never know it, but Stacey was a functioning drug addict. She'd been hooked on crack cocaine for the past year, borrowing money from time to time to support her habit. Shortly after leaving Sincere, she hit rock bottom and used the lethal drug as a getaway. In the beginning, she hid it from Brooklyn, knowing about her struggle with drugs in the past. She didn't want to be the reason that she got hooked. Eventually, it became harder, since Brooklyn was always around.

The basement was quiet and cold as Stacey pulled the cord connected to the light in the ceiling. Brooklyn didn't say a word as Stacey dug into a drawer and pulled out a plastic bag filled with glass vials of crack cocaine. She turned to Brooklyn and revealed the bag and the crack pipe, which she had in the same hand. Neither of them spoke as they both knew what was next. Brooklyn thought about turning around and walking out, but she desperately needed to escape the hell she was currently living in.

Before long Brooklyn felt an unimaginable feeling and completely forgot about the troubles at home. The high didn't last long, but the sickness she felt afterward was terrible. She vowed to steer clear of the drug because the short time span of the high didn't nearly outweigh the bout of sickness that followed.

Things between her and Jay weren't any better following that day, and the beatings became more brutal each time, so much so that she'd often be forced to run to Stacey and hide or be taken to the ER to be stitched up.

Depressed and desperately looking for a way out of the situation, she'd decided to give the drug one more try after Stacey promised her that she wouldn't be sick from it. Stacey explained that her lack of experience with the drug was what caused the sickness, that if she showed her how to use it properly, she'd be hooked. And that was exactly what happened.

Brooklyn, at rock bottom, was unable to resist. She finally found a way to survive, knowing there was something that could help. It wasn't the ideal situation or the wisest choice, but for some time it worked.

With the help of the drug, she was finally able to walk away from Jay and get on with her life. She planned on finding a new man, one who could appreciate her, knowing that hitting was out of the question.

Chapter Nineteen

On to the Next
1992

Brooklyn was excited about her date. She'd finally found someone who appeared to be a nice guy. After years of abuse and going back and forth with Jay, Sincere, and drugs, she felt good about the future. She believed that a good man would be the key to a full recovery. She didn't know what he had planned, but she was anxious all day, waiting for the time to come. She'd fixed her hair and makeup and sprayed some perfume on, hoping to excite him. She wasn't expecting to have sex, but she wanted to be prepared.

Once he arrived, she was even more excited to head out on the date. From what she remembered, Mike was a good-looking brother. Though she was still trying to get over Jay, she had learned from past experience to never get her hopes up too high too soon. She also swore to never allow herself to get played again.

"Wow! You look good!" he said, as she opened the door.

"Thanks," she replied. "So, where are we headed?" She anticipated enjoying herself and prayed that this date would turn out as expected.

"It's a surprise. Do you like surprises?" he asked, reaching his hand out for her to grab hold of it.

"I love surprises!" she admitted, before grabbing his hand and closing the door behind her.

They drove for what seemed like an eternity before arriving at a black-owned, Southern and Italian cuisine restaurant in New Jersey. She fell in love with it immediately.

Seated at the reserved table, Brooklyn thought the dim lighting and candle lights made the mood romantic. "This is a really nice restaurant, Mike. I'm impressed."

"Why? I don't look like a classy dude?" he asked with a smile.

"Oh, no. You look very classy. I just didn't expect you to bring me here on a first date. I'm sure it's really expensive, since the menus don't have prices on them." She laughed.

Joining in the laughter, Mike replied, "Damn! You noticed that? That's funny. But the money isn't an object for me." He had brought a bottle of Dom Perignon to the small, quiet, bring-your-own-bottle restaurant. "You're a beautiful lady, and I don't mind treating you well. Stick around, and you'll see I have a lot to offer."

Mike looked even better being suave. Though his words could have been genuine, it was hard for Brooklyn to believe what men said. He was turning her on, though, and if things went well, she would keep him around. Even if it was just to be a friend, he was good company.

"Well, I appreciate that, Mike," she said, smiling.

The food took an extremely long time to come, but while they waited, they brought out a sample of an appetizer, with red pepper, cheese, oils and crackers. She was at first turned off by the look of it and afraid to eat it.

It wasn't until the chef came out from the back to greet everyone that she gathered up the heart to try it.

How could I not try it with the chef standing there tell-ing me how good it is? she thought. Surprisingly it was really good, and she was glad that she'd tried it.

Dinner went off without a hitch, and soon they were heading out of the restaurant. She wondered what he had planned next. She was a little tipsy but could stand for a little more fun.

"So, where are we headed to now?" she asked, as she opened the passenger side door.

"I was going to take you home, but if you can think of somewhere else you'd like to go, I'm all for it."

"Why don't we go out to Penn's Landing and walk around, enjoy the night air?"

"At this time of night? Are you crazy?" He laughed.

"Yeah, maybe that's not such a good idea. I can't think of anything else to do. I just know that I'm not ready for this night to be over," she said as they both sat down in their seats.

"We can always go to my spot, if you'd like to," he said.

She gave him a quick stare and replied, "Your spot, huh?"

"I'm just saying . . . I can't think of anywhere else to go either."

"That's cool. We can go to your place."

"OK, then we are on our way," he replied, turning the car on.

Soon they were pulling up in front of his South Philly apartment. Brooklyn was nervous about going in for some reason. She didn't want him to get the wrong idea about her. It's not like she planned on having sex with him, but he was fine, she was tipsy, and it had been a while since she'd had some, so who knew what could happen?

Heading up the stairs to his second-floor apartment, she slowly followed behind him. She was shocked at how neat everything was inside his apartment. The place looked like no one lived there.

"Damn! It's so neat in here. Is this really your place?" she joked.

"Yeah, it's my place. I'm just a neat freak. Can't stand clutter and dirt."

"That's cool," she said as she took a look around. His color scheme was earth tone, browns and greens that blended nicely. He had brown leather furniture with cream stone tables and glass tops. He had a large-screen TV with a huge surround-sound system.

I could get used to coming over here, she thought. Everything about it felt so comfortable. She took a seat on the sofa and instantly took off her shoes.

"I see you don't waste time getting comfortable." Mike laughed.

"No, I don't."

He came over and sat next to her. She could feel the heat from his body. She wanted to get up and leave because the temptation was killing her. He turned to look at her, and she quickly turned away, embarrassed that she had been staring.

"What's wrong? What are you thinking about?"

"Nothing," she lied.

"Really, what are you thinking about?"

"I like you, Mike, and I didn't expect to."

"Damn! Well, at least you're honest."

"No, really. I had a crazy ending to my last relationship and was kind of bitter. I thought that I wouldn't let myself love or even like another person after being hurt. But you're a nice guy, and I couldn't take what someone else did out on you. I think we can be really good friends, and who knows what will happen next," she said, moving closer to him.

"Well, I'm glad you didn't, and I'm glad you like me, because I really like you," he said as he stared her in the eyes.

Brooklyn decided to just go with her heart and kiss him. She couldn't resist, with him licking his sexy-ass lips after each sentence. She knew he wouldn't turn her away, and she felt like being daring. She moved in and softly touched his lips with hers.

Mike returned the kiss and slowly placed his hands on her thighs.

Damn! He isn't wasting any time.

Mike moved his kisses from her lips to her neck, and she tilted her head to the side to give him more space, trying to control herself. Her panties were getting wet as he caressed her thighs and French-kissed her neck with slow, steady tongue movement.

"Stand up and undress," he ordered.

Brooklyn got up from the sofa and obeyed. As he watched her, he began to undress as well. She was glad to see that he was blessed down below when she saw his hard member standing at attention. In fact, her mouth was watering. If they'd known each other longer, she would have gotten down on her knees and put her tongue to work. She didn't want him to think that she just got down for anyone, so she held in the urge and instead let him take control.

"Turn around. I want to admire every inch of you."

Mike's demands were turning Brooklyn on. She couldn't let him know how excited she really was, but it was so hard not to. Every time she got a glimpse of his muscular, sexy, chocolate ass, she wanted to jump on him. Instead, she kept her cool and went along with it.

"Do you like what you see?" She had made a full circle and was now staring at him as he stood holding his hard dick in his hand.

He smiled when he noticed the look she gave him. "What's that look for? I didn't scare you, did I?"

"No, if it's one thing about me that's a fact. It's that I ain't never scared." She let out a girlish giggle.

"Well, come over here and get it then."

Brooklyn didn't waste any time, damn near running to make her way over to him. She was in desperate need of some sexual healing for sure. She stared him in the eye and met his lips with hers.

Mike's hands were around her waist, tickling the small of her back. His lips were softer than hers, and his rubbing against her made her more excited than she'd been about sex in a long time. She could just imagine those lips touching her pussy. She was sure to melt all over them.

They both were breathing heavily when he picked her up off the ground. She wrapped her long legs around him, and with ease he slid his dick inside of her pussy. She almost burst on contact. All of her adrenaline rushed to that spot, and as a moan escaped his mouth, her walls began to contract, gripping him like she was milking a cow. He held on to her ass and lifted it up each time she pushed down, fitting every inch of him in her tunnel. Together they created a flawless rhythm and an episode of mind-blowing intimacy that she wouldn't soon forget.

Mike stepped back toward the sofa, still holding her in the same position. Brooklyn loved a strong man. He'd had her in the air for the past fifteen minutes. She was soon lying down on the sofa with him on top of her, and they hadn't been separated for a second, while making the transition.

"Is it good to you, baby? I need to hear you speak."

She was enjoying herself too much to let out a word. Afraid she would lose her concentration and not be able to come, she lay there silent with her eyes closed until he stopped mid-stroke.

"What's wrong?" she asked.

"I mean, if you're not enjoying it, there's no reason to keep going," he replied with a devilish grin.

"Of course, I'm enjoying it. Don't you hear all the noise I'm making?"

"That could be an act."

"I'm not acting, OK. Now keep giving it to me, so I can show you exactly how much I'm enjoying it."

Mike smiled, and a few seconds later, he was pounding her again. Now, she was screaming, moaning, and yelling his name, amongst other things. She couldn't walk away from this without coming, so she had to perform as he wanted her to.

They were both dripping with sweat and breathing heavily, when she felt his body heating up. She palmed his ass to pull him in closer, and instantly her body began to shake and her juices were leaking out all over the sofa.

He followed right behind her, trembling. He quickly pulled out of her, grabbed hold of his dick, and released onto her stomach.

Brooklyn was a little grossed out by that, but not enough to change her mood. Hell, it was better that he put it there than let it out inside of her.

"Man, that was good." Mike wiped his forehead and sat down at the opposite end of the sofa.

Brooklyn was still lying flat on her back, one of her legs behind his back, the other across his lap. "Yes, it was." She laughed. "Where's your bathroom?"

"Straight up the steps to your left. Washcloths are in the cabinet."

As she peeled herself from the couch to walk toward the stairs, Mike smacked her on the ass, and she turned around and gave him a giggle.

Once she entered the bathroom and locked the door behind her, she grabbed a washcloth from the cabinet behind the door and turned on the sink. Of course, her instincts told her to look around. *Who wouldn't try and find out more about someone that they'd just met and screwed?* she thought.

Looking inside the medicine cabinet, she saw acne cream, cold medication, shaving cream. Then she noticed a prescription bottle with a female's name on it. *So he has a woman?* she thought. It's not like she had asked him, but why would he bring her into his home?

As she continued to search, more items stood out—a makeup kit on top of the counter, and a pink bottle of lotion under the sink. She wasn't angry, but she was a little annoyed. She decided not to let it show, not wanting to ruin the evening. She cleaned up and quietly headed back downstairs to get dressed.

"You want to stay the night, or you want me to drive you home?"

"You can drive me home. I have to get up pretty early in the morning," she lied. She didn't want someone to walk in on them and start an altercation.

"Cool. Let me go wipe off, and I'll take you."

Brooklyn grabbed her clothes from the floor and was dressed and ready to go in record time. Soon, they were on the expressway and sitting quietly.

Before leaving, they hugged, and she promised to call him the next day. She didn't believe that she would. It just seemed like the perfect thing to say at the time. She chose to end the night that way, to avoid talking about him belonging to someone else. To her, it not only meant that he was a cheater, but she also wouldn't be able to have him to herself.

Without that, there wasn't really any reason to move forward.

Chapter Twenty

First Impressions
1992

Months later Brooklyn was back on the dating scene. Her latest prospect was Tommy, a tall, light-skinned guy who worked in rehabilitation. She'd left Mike alone after their one-night stand after realizing he was already attached to someone. At this point in her life, she refused to play second fiddle to anyone.

"Hello!"

"Hello. Is Brooklyn there?"

"Speaking. Who is this?"

"This is Tommy."

"Oh! Hi, Tommy. I didn't think you were going to call me this soon." Brooklyn, pleasantly surprised, had a huge smile on her face. She'd met him a few days earlier. She was hesitant after her experience with Mike but figured she'd give dating one more try.

"I couldn't stop thinking about you from the first time I saw you," he blurted out.

"Well, why didn't you say anything to me?"

"I don't know. I guess I'm a little shy."

"What? Shy? I doubt it," she said, laughing

"Really, I thought you probably wouldn't want to talk to me." Tommy laughed too.

"Well, I definitely don't mean to be intimidating. I'm actually a very nice person, once you get to know me."

"Well, knowing you is what I want."

"That's what I want too."

"Well, what are you doing Friday night?"

"Nothing that I know of. Why?"

"How about I take you out somewhere special to start on that getting-to-know-each-other thing?"

"That's fine with me. What time?" Brooklyn was blushing and smiling so wide, you could see every tooth in her mouth.

"Probably around six, but I'll call you Thursday and let you know the exact time."

"OK. Then it's a date."

"Yes, it is. Well, have a good night."

"Goodnight, Tommy," she replied before hanging up.

Brooklyn couldn't wipe that big smile off of her face. *Maybe this could be the start of a new life,* she thought.

Friday couldn't come fast enough for her, but when it did, she was ready. She put on a knee-length black dress and a pair of black shoes. When the doorbell rang, she instantly got butterflies in her stomach. He looked even better than before, dressed in a black suit.

Damn! A suit surely makes a difference, she thought. He looked like he'd just stepped off the pages of *GQ* magazine.

"You look beautiful." Tommy smiled, looking her up and down.

She returned the smile. "You don't look too bad yourself."

"Thanks."

After a few minutes of small talk, they were on their way. Brooklyn was surprised to see he was driving a Mercedes Benz. She knew UPS workers made good money, but she didn't think it was that good.

He took her to a beautiful restaurant. Then they danced. He smelled so good and was so damn fine, almost perfect in her book.

She saw he had a little smirk on his face. "So what are you thinking about?" she asked softly.

"I can't believe such a beautiful woman is actually giving me a chance."

"Well, how about if I told you that I felt the same way?"

"I would be flattered. But I know handsome men come at you all the time."

"Well, I have been through a lot with men. It seems like every man I have been with in my entire life did me wrong."

"I'm sorry to hear that. I can't understand what would possibly make someone want to hurt you."

"I don't either, but the fact of the matter is, they do, and that's not a route I'm trying to take again."

"Well, if you let me into your life, I promise you I won't hurt you."

At that moment she remembered the way she felt when she and Sincere were first together. The feeling was similar. She looked at Tommy and felt like she could love him, but she wasn't sure if her heart was ready. She wanted to kiss him but held back, not knowing how he would react.

After they took a walk outside and talked some more, he drove her home. He didn't ask or try to kiss her; he just assured her that he would see her soon.

Brooklyn went in and closed the door, smiled, exhaled, and rested her back against the door. She felt like this was the start of something wonderful and was looking forward to what would happen next.

Chapter Twenty-one

Serious
1993

Brooklyn couldn't have been more excited. Her body was yearning for some attention, and Tommy was just the man to give it to her. She wanted to make love to him, though she did think it was too soon. She didn't want him to get the wrong idea about her. She sat there debating if tonight would be the night.

Fuck it! she thought. There wasn't any turning back from this point. She needed him and was surely going to show him how much. She figured if she asked him to come back later on after he finished working and stay the night with her, he'd get the point.

The doorbell rang about twenty minutes later, and instantly butterflies were fluttering in her stomach. She slowly opened the door, a huge smile on her face.

"Hey, beautiful." He smiled as he passed her a bouquet of flowers.

Even though Brooklyn thought it was a little corny, she still thought it was really cute. It was one of the nicest things a man had ever done for her, which didn't say a lot for the jerks she'd dealt with in the past.

"For me?" she asked, as if she didn't already know. "These are so nice, Tommy. I really appreciate that."

"I figured I could show you a little token of appreciation for going out with me."

"You being here was enough." Brooklyn headed to the kitchen to put the flowers down.

When she turned around, Tommy was standing right in front of her, their faces almost touching. Her body was quivering, and she couldn't even speak. Soon his lips met hers, and they engaged in a long, passionate kiss.

Brooklyn could feel his hands moving down the small of her back, toward the base of her spine. She wanted him to go farther, but she had to stop him. She wanted their first time to be perfect. She knew that might sound like a fairy tale, but hell, it was *her* fairy tale.

She pulled away and looked him in the eye. He appeared unsure about taking the next step. She quickly told him, "I've dreamed about this moment for so long, and it felt a hundred times better than I could have imagined."

"So why did you stop me?" He backed away.

"Because I want things to be perfect. I know you have to go back to work. A quickie won't do." She laughed, trying to bring some humor to the situation. "But, really, I want you to come back here after you're done for the evening and rub me all night long."

Tommy left with a smile on his face. He returned with a plan. Instead of staying there that evening, he took her to a hotel equipped with a hot tub and all. Brooklyn had never been to such a posh hotel.

As soon as they arrived, he started kissing her. When she didn't resist, he began to slide his tongue into her mouth. She pulled him inside of the bedroom area and wrapped her arms around him.

Tommy untied her dress, revealing her nakedness underneath. Her nipples became instantly erect as he rubbed his hands across them. He grabbed hold of her ass, and her stiff nipple pressed against his shirt. He was excited about making love to her, and even if this was the last time, he believed it was worth the trouble of driving all the way over there to the hotel.

He eased her down to the floor in the hallway, and as she lay on top of her dress that had fallen to the plush carpet, he stared at her body, which was much more beautiful than he'd imagined, her skin as smooth as a newborn baby's.

Her pussy was wet to the touch, and with her legs spread-eagled, he lay flat on his stomach to plant a French kiss on it. The taste was wonderful, and as her juices filled his mouth, she began to moan loudly.

After she had her first orgasm, he quickly took off his pants and lay on the floor. Crossing their legs, he moved close, so he could ease his dick inside of her. They immediately began grinding against each other, and it wasn't long before she erupted and began shaking. Anxious to release more of his energy, he got up and let her go to the hot tub.

After running the water, both of them climbed inside. Sitting on opposite sides of the hot tub, they could feel their temperatures rising far above the hot water.

Tommy licked his lips in anticipation at Brooklyn's round breasts, which sat just above the water. He slowly moved his hands down to his throbbing dick and began to stroke it. Through the rising steam, she watched as he pleasured himself with his eyes on her.

"Do you want me to taste you again?" he quizzed. She seemed anxious to be touched.

Brooklyn nodded her head yes, and he moved close to her, her hard nipples touching his chest as their lips met, and they instantly began to massage each other's tongues. The sweet taste of her lip gloss excited him as he moved his hands down to her wet pussy. She moaned as he slowly slid one finger at a time deep inside of her, and the warmth of her tunnel sent him wild.

He moved his kisses from her lips to her neck, and she tilted her neck to the side to give him full access. The scent of her perfume turning her on, he continued to tickle her clit.

"Bend over," he said.

Brooklyn bent over so that her ass was facing him, her erect nipples touching the water.

Tommy started caressing her perfectly round ass, which was just waiting to be kissed, and soon he was planting French kisses all over it. He stiffened his tongue and began to massage her asshole, which was delivering sweet nectar to his taste buds, holding on to her waist, forcing his tongue deep inside, until she couldn't take anymore.

Next Brooklyn sat on the edge of the hot tub with her legs opened wide. Her juicy mound was like art that deserved delicate attention. He got down on his knees and stared at her wetness as she held her lips open for him, and slowly licked her clit, making figure eight with his thick tongue over and over and sending her wild. Then he sucked on her wet clit and slowly let it slip from his lips a few times before burying his face deep inside.

While he was making love to her with his tongue, she was palming the back of his head for a deeper grind. She began to tremble as she reached her peak yet again. But Tommy kept going and sucked up all of the come that she released.

Brooklyn sat on the edge of the hot tub exhausted, but more than willing to return the favor.

Tommy was ready as he stood up over her. With one leg over her shoulder, he rocked his hips back and forth and made love to her face as she began to suck on his hard dick.

"Right there!" he moaned. He enjoyed letting his juices run down her chin. "Keep sucking, baby!" he yelled as he neared an orgasm. It wasn't long before he was coming, and barely able to stand.

Afterward, Tommy sat down next to Brooklyn, while she licked her lips. The experience was so special, neither of them could come up with a word to describe how good they felt.

Chapter Twenty-two

Hitting the Fan
1993

"Where are you going?" Tommy hollered from the rear of the apartment.

"I have to make a few stops." Just then, Brooklyn snuck into his coat pocket and peeled off forty dollars, hoping he wouldn't miss it. "I'll be back shortly."

"All right. Well, pick me up something to eat on your way back."

"OK," she replied, though she had other plans that surely didn't involve food. She walked out of the door, and to the corner where Stacey was waiting for her.

"Did you get it?" Stacey asked.

"Yeah, I got it. Let's go."

The two turned the corner and began the six-block walk to their destination, a small row home where they'd be able to purchase the drugs they were looking for. With the money Brooklyn had stolen from Tommy, she and Stacey could buy a four-day supply of heroin and cocaine. As they did on most days, they would go inside and get high and try to maintain their normal lives. If Brooklyn couldn't steal cash from Tommy, she would steal items and sell them to support her habit. She didn't care who it came from or what she had to do to get it. Of course, with so much drug use, she had become thin and frail.

The two patiently waited in line for their product and hurried to the corner to prepare to get high. After leaving the house they roamed the streets. Most days they would walk for hours and accomplish nothing.

Meanwhile, Brooklyn's mother and children were living in a condemned home. Part of the roof had fallen in, and there was no gas. They were sharing a room that they used to do pretty much everything. They would bathe and even cook on an electric hot plate in the same room that they'd all cuddle up and sleep in. Brooklyn occasionally popped in and out but not often enough. Most of her visits led to fistfights with her mother and arguments with her oldest daughter.

Brooklyn headed back to the house empty-handed, forgetting all about the food Tommy had asked for, and entered calmly.

"Where the fuck is my money, Brooklyn?"

"What money?"

"You know what money I'm talking about," he yelled. "Forty dollars is missing out of my coat." Tommy was aware of Brooklyn's drug habit in the past but had been fooled into thinking she had quit. Lately, money was missing and bills weren't getting paid, so he already assumed she'd been using the money to get high. Deep down, he was hoping it wasn't true, that she was actually using the money for something else.

She stood there trying to come up with an answer, the effects of the drugs she'd used earlier having worn off. "I don't know what you're talking about, Tommy. I don't have any of your money."

"Oh, yeah? Well, clear your pockets."

"What?"

"You heard me. Clear your pockets and show me what's inside." He moved in closer to her, breathing hard on her face.

"I'm a grown-ass woman, Tommy. I'm not clearing shit. I already told you I didn't take your fucking money. Now back up," she yelled, nudging him away.

"I know you're out there getting high again. I told you, if I found out about it, you were getting out. I'm not living with no fucking junkie, you hear me?"

"I just told you I'm not getting high."

Tommy pushed her onto the sofa and sat on top of her, holding her arms down. As she tried to resist, he dug in her pockets and pulled out the bags of heroin she had inside.

Waving the bags in the air, he looked at her with hatred, wondering how the hell he'd fallen for her in the first place. "You're not on anything? Then what the hell is this?"

"Get off of me, Tommy! I'm not going to sit here and argue with you. If you want me gone, then fine, I'm gone."

Tommy stood off her and let her rise from the sofa, and she headed to the back room to attempt to gather her belongings. He stormed into the room behind her, snatching the bag from her hand.

"You're not taking anything of mine. Everything that I paid for is staying here."

She frowned her face up before turning to leave the room. She knew he'd come looking for her as he normally did, begging her to come back, so she walked out without any hesitation.

Within a week she was right back home, and back to stealing his money every chance she got, so she could go out and run the streets.

She was slowed down a great deal, once she learned that she was once again pregnant. She was pissed that she had to deal with the responsibility of a baby once again. She was absent in her children's life and didn't fight to change it, so she knew the same thing would happen with this one. She even contemplated abortion but was certain if she got her hands on that type of money, getting rid of the baby would be the last thing on her mind.

Tommy wasn't too excited, but he was hoping that a baby would be just the thing she needed to slow her down. As much as he begged her to stop getting high for the sake of the baby, it still didn't matter one bit.

Of course, with a woman like Brooklyn, there was no winning when she had her mind set on doing something. She wasn't ready to quit and didn't plan on it anytime soon. Months into the pregnancy she was still running the streets. She was barely gaining weight and would oftentimes get sick when she got high, but would still look for more once her stomach settled.

A few weeks short of her delivery, she attempted to take a break, hoping the drugs in her system would go unnoticed. She didn't realize that her baby would experience withdrawal symptoms as well. She ended up right back on the drugs to avoid getting sick.

After a long day on the streets, she realized that her water had broken, and she was rushed to the hospital in more pain than she could remember being in. Even being high didn't mask the pain.

She cursed almost everyone she came in contact with during the delivery, including Tommy, who arrived an hour after she'd gotten there. Stacey, who had been with her the whole day, was at her side, trying to calm her. She gave birth to a boy, who was instantly taken to the newborn intensive care unit to be treated. The baby was hooked on the drugs his mother used daily, had respiratory problems, and an extremely fast heart rate.

After weeks of intensive care, Tommy Jr. was allowed to go home with his dad. Since Brooklyn wasn't living at Tommy's house, he was granted custody after a complete background check.

After the baby was home, Brooklyn spent a lot of time with him, but it became stressful and couldn't keep her still. During the day she would run the streets and go there at night, staying up with the baby all night, while Tommy worked. Life with the baby wasn't something she was used to or even wanted to get used to.

Meanwhile, Tommy struggled and was becoming more fed up with each passing day.

Chapter Twenty-three

Keep On Walking
1994

"How's the baby?" Tommy asked as he entered the living room.

"He's fine," she snapped.

"Why all the attitude tonight?"

"Tommy, please don't start."

"Don't tell me what the hell to do. I asked you a question!"

"Nothing, Tommy. I'm just tired. I have a newborn baby that keeps me up all night. I guess you wouldn't know, because you're never here."

"What did you say? Don't blame me for him keeping you up. If your ass wasn't a crackhead, he'd be fine, so you can't blame anyone but yourself for that one."

"Forget it, Tommy. I'm in no mood to argue with you tonight."

"Well, guess what, Brooklyn? You don't make the fucking rules! I pay the bills in here, so I'll talk about what I want when I want," Tommy said, grabbing her arm tightly.

"Tommy, you're hurting my arm."

"I don't care, and unless you plan on stopping me—"

"Calm down. You're going to wake the baby up."

"I told you not to tell me what to do, didn't I?"

"Tommy!" she screamed.

"Fuck you, OK!" He spat in her face and walked toward the door.

Brooklyn broke down as she wiped his spit from her face. She had never been so disrespected in her entire life. *Why me?* she thought. *Why is this happening to me?*

Instead of looking in the mirror at the true cause, Brooklyn never accepted responsibility for her mistakes and often blamed everyone else when things went wrong. She knew their relationship was pretty much done at this point, but now that a baby was involved, it wasn't as simple to walk away as she'd done with him many times in the past.

Tired of worrying about his attitude, or the times when the baby needed to eat, she was ready to be on her own. She knew what people thought of her, but she didn't care. After Tommy left, she put the baby to sleep, got dressed, and left a note that she wouldn't be back.

Tommy returned to the house an hour later to find the baby still asleep and Brooklyn missing. He searched the house thinking that she'd possibly just fallen asleep in another room, since she'd claimed she was tired. After returning to the room where the baby was sleeping, he found her note. He sat down on the edge of the bed staring at it and shaking his head in disbelief. He realized at that moment that, regardless of how hard she'd tried, she was never gonna be the woman he fell in love with. He had to give up on her if he was going to be a good father to his son.

Brooklyn had just arrived at Stacey's house, and as she waited for her to open the door, she thought about the life she was leaving behind. She was sure Tommy and the baby would be better off without her.

Stacey opened the door with a smile. "Girl, what are you doing here?"

"I left them," she replied, walking into the house.

"You left who?"

"Tommy and the baby."

"What do you mean you left them?"

"I walked out. I left a note telling him I wasn't coming back. I'm tired, Stacey, and I can't do it no more. I can't sit around always worrying about someone else. I need to think about me."

"You don't really mean that, Brooklyn."

"Why not? I mean, look at me, Stacey—I look like shit and I have kids I don't even think about. No one needs me. They are all better off without me."

"That's not true, Brooklyn. They do need you. Hell, I need you. Remember when we talked about getting clean together? I think now is the time. We both had bright futures and let the streets ruin it. I think they'll all be able to forgive you if you get your life back on track."

"I don't think they'll ever forgive me, and I deserve it. I treated my family like shit. I was always addicted to something, you know. Before drugs there were men and money, and they were just as damaging to me. There's no reason to quit, because there's nothing to live for anymore."

"Look, I know you're just upset, so you're saying things that you don't mean, but I know how it feels to be down, and on top as well. We can't sit thinking about the things we could've had. We have to think about what we currently have and the things we want to get."

Brooklyn sat there taking in every word, yet she was feeling like she wasn't strong enough to make a step toward getting better, like a mere pawn in a game she could never win.

Chapter Twenty-four

They Keep Calling
1996

Brooklyn stood in the mirror looking at herself as she prepared to go see her family. She'd been running the streets and hadn't seen her children in almost a year. She wanted to look as presentable as possible when she showed her face, to spare herself as much embarrassment as she could. She wasn't really enthusiastic about stopping in but felt it was about time that she went.

It was mid-morning when she left Stacey's house to head over. The weather was cold, but she was bundled up enough to shield herself from the wind that almost blew her over when she tried to cross a street. She hadn't seen Stacey since the night before, so she stopped by their local hotspot on the way, just to let her know where she'd be for the evening. As she walked toward the house she spotted some commotion in the alley a couple of feet from the house. She glanced over but knew not to stick her nose in other people's business, especially in that neighborhood.

Right as she walked past the alley, she heard a scream from a voice that sounded like Stacey's. She then walked over to see what all the fuss was about.

"Stacey," she called out as she walked closer. She couldn't see her through the crowd but could hear her sobs a mile away. She called out her name again, pushing her way through the crowd.

Once she made it to the front of the group, she found Stacey on her hands and knees, leaning over a man's lifeless body. She couldn't see who it was, but something told her she knew the man. She called Stacey's name again, grabbing a hold of her shoulder, so she could see who it was. She almost fainted when she saw Sincere's face.

She got down next to Stacey and grabbed hold of Sincere's blood-soaked shirt, trying to shake him, but he wasn't moving. He was already gone, but neither of them was ready to believe that.

"Come on, Sincere, get up," Brooklyn said, shaking him repeatedly.

Sincere had been shot the night before and left in the alley, hence the reason for the dried up blood on his clothes. A man who had gone in the alley to urinate saw his motionless body and screamed, causing the group to form. The bystanders looked on as the two women cried over the man they loved, a man who'd fathered a child by both women.

"What happened? What the hell happened to him?" Brooklyn screamed into the crowd, while Stacey was sitting there in a daze, tears pouring down her cheeks.

Brooklyn couldn't believe her eyes and was hoping it was all a dream. Though they'd had a tumultuous relationship, she'd always loved him and never wanted to see him hurt. Everyone standing around was acting as if they had no clue, when they probably knew a whole lot more.

Soon she heard the cops pulling up and entering the alley, pushing everyone away from the scene, including herself and Stacey, who had to be practically pried away from his body.

Both women knew that, with the life he lived, there was a strong possibility that someone would try to get rid of him. Now that the situation was staring them right in the face, they were having a hard time coping with it, even though he wasn't much of a father to their kids. Brooklyn stood the stronger of the two, holding it together, as the officer spread a sheet over his dead body.

Sidney pulled up a few moments later and was trying to bust through the police tape to see Sincere's body, but the officers guarding the area denied him access. He quickly got back in his car and sped off.

Brooklyn's plan of going to see her family had now changed. She wasn't prepared to tell Sasha that her father had been murdered. She decided on taking Stacey home. The remainder of the day she sat staring out the window, a million questions running through her head, as Stacey lay in a blanket on the couch. She wondered who the culprit was and imagined taking them out for what they'd done.

The following day Brooklyn broke the news to her daughter, who took it hard. She wanted to make sure to be there for her, totally ignoring the fact that she needed someone as well.

Brooklyn had never lost anyone she'd cared about, so she didn't know how to deal with her loss. She cried often but would straighten up to be the backbone for everyone else, using drugs to take her mind off the situation. Slowly it was eating away at her, feeling like she couldn't talk to anyone. Now she'd turned into someone unlovable, even to herself, and wasn't sure how to handle it. The more she thought about it, the more depressed she became. She remembered her life before Sincere and how bad she wanted to grow up. She often wondered, if she hadn't gotten with him, would her life have been any different?

Brooklyn often found herself walking around just to get some air. This day, as she walked across the small bridge, she looked out into the water and thought about ending it all. Again, she thought about how much better off everyone would be without her.

She stood looking over the gate into the water, and after a few more moments of sulking, she suddenly climbed the gate and jumped into the cold water, breaking through the thin-layered sheet of ice that covered it.

Brooklyn woke up was and found herself in a hospital bed. She looked around the room and noticed Stacey sitting in a chair on the opposite side of the room. She sat up slowly, feeling disoriented.

"Girl, if you ever scare me like that again, I'll kill you!" Stacey laughed. "What the hell were you thinking?"

"Honestly, I was just thinking how I didn't want to be here anymore." She felt a tear streaming down her face. "I don't know why God keeps sparing me, Stacey. I just want it to be over."

"He keeps sparing you, because it's not your time. You can try to kill yourself in a million different ways, but if He's not ready for you, you'll still be here, Brooklyn. We all have a purpose in life, regardless of how blinded we may be. You just have to try and push through the heartache to see it. I mean, look at us—You hated me once, and we've become best friends again. I know you can get through anything."

Brooklyn looked up at Stacey and realized how wise she'd become over the years. She'd matured much more than she had. She was glad she had someone like her around to look out for her when things were bad.

Stacey looked down at her friend and remembered the vibrant girl she once was. She realized she had to fight for both of them if Brooklyn was going to make it through. She hated seeing her so depressed. Instead of drilling her with more insight, she decided to climb in bed with her and hold her hand.

"Do you remember when we were young? I think we were about nine or ten, and you had that little dog that would never stop barking. Well, I remember the day the dog got hit by a car and you cried and cried, thought your life was over. Then, come to find out, it wasn't even your dog." Stacey laughed. "I was right there holding your hand, girl, and I'm still here for you."

Brooklyn lay next to Stacey, barely awake, tears slowly falling from her eyes. She realized how much Stacey cared for her. If she ever needed a reason to fight and get better, she had one now.

Chapter Twenty-five

One More Chance
1997

The street was dark and quiet as Brooklyn crept down the small block. Everyone seemed fast asleep. She had a plan to execute that night—Climb into the first open window and take any valuables in sight. She'd rarely stolen from a stranger, but it was becoming harder to get things from her relatives, since most of them wouldn't leave her in a room alone in their houses.

She noticed a window halfway open. After cutting the screen, she took a look inside to make sure no one was occupying the room. Comfortable that the coast was clear, she stuck one leg in at a time and stepped on to the carpet. She began rummaging through the things she saw lying around in plain view. *Nothing of value here.*

She opened drawers and finally found a watch and a few dollars inside the desk, which was off to the far side of the wall. Walking to the opposite side of the room, she spotted a wallet, but just as she prepared to grab it, she saw a light come on in the rear of the house. She quickly ran toward the window to attempt to climb out.

A male voice yelled, "You muthafucka!" The man had a gun pointed in her direction.

She was struggling to get out of the window when she felt a burning in her leg. She fell out of the window and hit the ground hard. She'd been shot, and the pain was unbearable. She tried to crawl away, but the owner ran out of the house and was standing over her as she lay there in agony.

"You think you can steal from me and get away with it? You fucking crackhead! I should kill your ass for disrespecting me!" he screamed, the gun pointed in her face.

Brooklyn shook her head, her hands covering her face, hoping he wouldn't shoot her again. She could feel the blood pouring out of her leg, which was getting more numb by the second. She said a silent prayer, thinking her life was about to come to an end.

The man walked away and entered his home, where he dialed the police to report what had just occurred.

Brooklyn turned onto her stomach and tried to pull herself away from the house, afraid that he'd come back out and shoot her again. She'd left a trail of blood down the street to where she managed to drag herself.

Within five minutes the police arrived and the ambulance thereafter. Brooklyn, by that point, had passed out from the tremendous loss of blood. They put her into the ambulance and carted her off to the hospital as a Jane Doe, because she had no identification.

She was taken into surgery as soon as she arrived at the hospital. The bullet had shattered her left tibia, and the surgeons decided to insert a metal rod into her leg to repair it. Her rehabilitation would require months of physical therapy.

Brooklyn woke up, looking around, trying to figure out where she was, and what the hell happened to her. Her leg was suspended in the air and completely wrapped up, and her arm handcuffed to the bed. She thought for sure it was a nightmare.

Confused as to why, again, her life had been spared, she thought, *What the hell am I supposed to be doing?*

An Asian nurse entered the room a few moments later to check Brooklyn's vital signs and noticed she was awake. "How are you feeling?" she asked.

"Like shit! What did they do to my leg?"

"You had surgery. Your leg was shattered from the gunshot wound. Now that you're awake, I need to get some information from you. You didn't have any ID on you, so we couldn't contact anyone on your behalf."

"My name is Brooklyn . . . Brooklyn Johnson. And please don't call anyone. I don't want anyone to see me like this."

"No problem, Ms. Johnson. I'll go get the rest of the forms to fill out. Do you need anything else from me while I'm going out?"

"No, I'm fine."

Brooklyn looked out into the hallway and spotted a police officer talking to the nurse who had just walked out of the room. She'd already figured that she was under arrest for breaking into the man's house. She thought about calling Stacey, who she knew would be worried sick about her, but she wasn't prepared for the speech that would come with it. She also knew that if she didn't call her, she'd be furious. She was fighting with herself because she wasn't sure whether or not she'd be able to stand the look of disappointment on Stacey's face.

A few hours later, she decided to call her. She felt that, in the event things got worse, at least the one person who fought for her would know about it.

Stacey arrived at the hospital an hour later.

"Girl, we have to stop meeting like this—I can't stand hospitals. Girl, what the hell happened? Your leg is jacked up?"

"I got shot, girl. They say my leg was completely shattered."

"So that means you gonna be a cripple and shit?" Stacey laughed. "I'm just joking, girl. But damn! Where the hell were you? I told you stop trying to cop without me."

"Well, hey, if I hadn't, it would've probably been you in the bed next to me, so I'm glad I did."

"Shit. You could've been dead. I told you I'm not ready for you to leave me yet, all right. I brought you something too." She looked over her shoulder to watch out for the officer before going in her pocket and retrieving a small bag of cocaine.

"What am I gonna do with that, with the damn watchdog out there?"

"Don't worry. I'll distract him. Here, take it. I know you need it." Stacey passed her the bag before turning to walk to the door.

As Stacey flirted with the cop, Brooklyn opened the bag, scooped out some with her fingernail, and snorted it. After doing this routine four times, she closed the bag and stuck it under her pillow, coughing to signal Stacey.

After a few minutes she felt like herself. She always got depressed when she wasn't under the influence of drugs. It was those times when she thought about taking her own life. Stacey had come in and saved the day once again and made sure to be there through her rehab as well.

Luckily Brooklyn was able to skip going to jail, since she didn't have any priors. So it wasn't long before she was home. She knew it wouldn't be long before the call of the streets pulled her back in.

Chapter Twenty-six

A New Day
1998

"Brooklyn, is that you?" Mesa yelled as she spotted Brooklyn walking toward her mom's house.

Feeling ashamed, Brooklyn tried to turn away, but Mesa pulled over and jumped out of her car. Brooklyn's hair was all over the place, her clothing was loose and torn in different areas, and she walked with a limp.

"Brooklyn! It's me, Mesa!"

"I know," she said dryly.

"Oh my gosh! I thought you were dead. I ride by here all the time when I'm in the city, hoping I'll run into you," she said, looking at her once beautiful prospect. She was sad that she hadn't been able to protect her. "How have you been?"

"How does it look like I've been?" she asked.

Brooklyn hadn't spoken to Mesa in years. She could only feel that if they'd given her just one more shot, her life wouldn't have gotten so out of control. At one point she felt like Mesa was family, but she also felt betrayed when Mesa no longer supported her.

Mesa looked at her and wanted so badly to help to make up for not being there years ago when she really needed her. "Can I take you to grab something to eat? I just want to talk and catch up."

Brooklyn looked her up and down. She noticed her name-brand shoes and expensive clothes. She realized it could've been her in that attire, and not the old sweats and sneakers. She wondered what she'd accomplish by going to eat with her. But then she thought that Mesa probably felt guilty, and if nothing else, she might leave with a few dollars in her pocket.

"OK, I'll go."

"Great. Hop in." Mesa smiled and walked around to the driver's side of the car.

The two headed over to a small restaurant and sat down. Most of the patrons looked at the duo, mainly Brooklyn, and wondered how the hell they even knew each other. Brooklyn was unfazed, only anxious to get the meeting over with so she could get out of there and head to her destination.

"First, I want to start by apologizing to you. I feel so bad about the way things turned out for you. I feel like I should've done more."

"Let me stop you right there, because I don't need your sympathy. I didn't come here for that."

"I'm sorry if I offended you, but that was something I've wanted to say for years, and I've finally gotten a chance to do so. I remember the day I first saw you. You reminded me so much of myself. Trust and believe, I made all of the same mistakes that you did, even with the drugs, but I had someone there to support me. And that's where I failed with you."

"So what's the point? I mean, all of this reminiscing is depressing. We both know that none of this shit matters because now I'm just a run-down drug addict. It's nothing that you can do for me. I'm over. Any career that I had is long gone, so what is it that you want from me?"

"I just want to be there for you. If you need anything, I want you to be able to pick up the phone and know that I'm there."

"Sounds good, but the reality is, you weren't there for me before. So why would you be there for me now?"

"Because this is a new me, Brooklyn. I'm trying to do right. I feel like your downfall was my fault. You wouldn't have ever been a model without me, and you would have never met Natasha if it weren't for me either. Which means you probably would've never started doing drugs if it weren't for me."

"Well, I guess we'll never know, will we? And speaking of Natasha, how is she?"

Mesa paused, knowing what she was going to say next wouldn't be taken well.

Brooklyn sat there staring at her, waiting for her reply, feeling like something was wrong.

"She died, Brooklyn. Over a year ago she died from an overdose."

Brooklyn laughed. She didn't truly believe that Mesa was telling the truth. After a few seconds, she realized that Mesa's facial expression hadn't changed.

"Why didn't anyone tell me? I mean, damn, she was one of my best friends, and I wasn't even told about the funeral."

"I tried to find you, Brooklyn, I really did. I went to your mom's house. I thought it was abandoned. I didn't have any way to contact you, so I figured I would tell you once I was able to sit down and talk to you face to face."

"I just can't believe it. She was doing so good. I thought she quit, and she was still getting high." Brooklyn shook her head in disbelief.

The waitress came to the table to take their order. Brooklyn ordered enough food to take some home. After hearing the bad news about her friend, she was in no mood to eat.

"So when you say *anything*, do you really mean *anything*?"

"Yes, just let me know what you need."

"If you could help me out with a few dollars, that would help a lot."

"If you promise me that you'll use it for something other than drugs, no problem. I'm just really trying to help you, Brooklyn. I want to see you get back on your feet.

"Well, I appreciate that." Brooklyn realized she had to play the game if she wanted the money she needed. "I mean, believe me, I hated your guts. I've been let down by everyone in my life—my father, mother, men, and then you. I really depended on you. I can honestly agree with you on something."

"What's that?"

"That it was your fault."

Mesa sat there staring at Brooklyn. She didn't expect her to be so honest. "I can respect that, Brooklyn, and I'm so glad that you're able to be honest."

"*Honest* is definitely me."

"Well, again, I'm here to help, so whatever you need, just let me know."

After they left the restaurant, Mesa gave Brooklyn her business card as she dropped her off, and two hundred dollars, which was much more than she expected. She couldn't wait to get back to Stacey to show her.

Chapter Twenty-seven

Decisions
2000

Two years later Brooklyn was still doing her thing. She hadn't found anything worth changing for. Even looking at all of the damage she'd done to herself couldn't change anything. Inside she felt nothing, and as many times as you'd tell her how she'd ruined her life and those around her, she remained the same. As many times as she'd faced death, she still hadn't figured out her purpose.

Recently she had been spending time with her daughter, trying to be there for her. She'd started seeing in her some of the same things that she saw in herself.

It was a Saturday, which was normally the day they spent together, and Brooklyn was dressed and ready to go see her when she realized that Stacey wasn't feeling good. While Sasha sat patiently waiting for her, she was home playing nurse for her best friend. By the time she made it over to her mom's, Sasha was asleep. Her mother Janice wasn't too happy because she had to sit for an hour soothing Sasha until she actually fell asleep.

"What the hell are you here for?" Janice sipped her drink.

"To see my children. I'm damn sure not here to see you."

"Your children are asleep. You know I sat for an hour trying to console her. Why the fuck you even bother, if you aren't going to stand by what you say?"

"Like you have room to talk. What do you know about being a mother? Hell, I remember being more of a mother to the boys than you ever were."

"Maybe, but now that you have your own, you ain't shit! You had them for what reason? All you did was dump them on me."

"I'm surely not going to sit here and explain myself to you. Where is Sasha? I'm done with this conversation."

"You're not done. You're in my house, remember?"

"House? Is that what four walls make?"

"You know what? Fuck you, Brooklyn! You always talking shit about me, and you ain't nothing but a fiend. You think your kids don't know what you do? Imagine how they feel when people ask about you. You ever think about that? I don't give a damn how you feel about me, but you need to care about them. You see what happened to you."

As much as Brooklyn hated to admit it, she knew that her mother was part of the blame for her mistakes as well, and she didn't want her kids to grow up with the same hatred she felt for her mother. She wanted to be on time and hated standing Sasha up, but Stacey would have done the same thing for her, so she felt like she had no other choice. She believed if she did right by them, eventually they would get over it. She knew she had to do something.

She walked away from the argument and went up to the room where the kids were all sleeping in one bed. She kicked off her shoes and climbed in bed with them. The next morning they all woke up and finally spent some quality time together. She started to believe that now was a better time than any to make a major change.

Chapter Twenty-eight

Dreams
2000

Brooklyn sat in the room staring at the wall, waiting for Tommy to arrive. He'd been nice enough to meet with her to discuss their son. She hadn't seen nor heard from him since the day she'd walked out and was hoping he'd allow her back into their son's life. He probably hated her for the way things turned out between them, but at this point, it was no longer about what they had or could've had but more about what she could have with their child.

Tommy walked into the room dressed to kill as usual, not even a strand of hair in his mustache was out of place. He walked over to the table with a straight face, not cracking even the slightest smile, which to Brooklyn, showed that he meant business. She stood to hug him once he made it to the table. The hug felt like one from a stranger. She realized that any feelings he had for her had vanished.

"So what's up?" he said nonchalantly as he sat down in the chair opposite her.

"It's good to see you, Tommy. I know you may not believe it, but I always wanted the best for you and the baby. I really thought leaving was the best thing for both of you."

"It's not really about the past; I'm just trying to figure out what it is you plan to do now. I mean, you haven't seen him since he was a baby, so I'm really confused about you even asking me to come here."

"I know you'll never forget what I did, Tommy, but I'm hoping that one day you'll be able to forgive me. I meant well. I really did. I wasn't ready to be a mother to any of my children, and now it's like it's too late. I just want to be able to see him from time to time just to know that he's OK. I know that we'll probably never have a tight bond because of my decisions, but any relationship is better than none."

"Well, what makes you think he wants to see you? I mean, I'm not going to force him to see you and spend time with you if that's not what he wants to do. He has no clue who you are. He actually believes that you're dead . . . because to me, the day you walked out, you were. And if you're going to pop in and out of his life, then sorry, I can't allow you to see him."

"I'm not planning to pop in and out of his life, Tommy. I've really changed. A lot of things that weren't important to me in the past are very dear to me now. I knew when I left that there was a possibility I'd never see him again, and back then that was fine. I was sick, and it wouldn't have done him any good. I'm still struggling, but I'm just in a much better place now."

"So you're still getting high?"

Brooklyn sat there knowing the truth could possibly ruin any chance she had of getting back in her son's life, but she had to be honest with Tommy if she ever wanted him to trust her enough to give a little.

She took a deep breath. "Yes, but I plan to go to rehab very soon. You remember my agent Mesa? Well, she's been real helpful, and she found this great rehab for me to go to."

"I can't see how I can trust you, Brooklyn, when I'm not even sure that you're ready to change. You tell me you've changed, but I don't see it. I still see the same drug addict that walked out on us. You left a baby asleep in a crib alone with a note attached to him, Brooklyn. That's a lot to deal with, and every time I think about it, I get pissed. I remember waiting for the day that I could curse you for what you did, but eventually I had to let it go, so I could be there for him."

"I know it won't be easy, but if you could give me just one chance, I promise I will make you a believer. If not, then you'll never know what could've come from it. Things happen for a reason, Tommy. Just imagine the kind of havoc I would have wreaked if I'd stayed. You would've probably really hated me then."

"I don't hate you, Brooklyn, I really don't. I always wanted the best for you. I wanted the best for us. I really don't feel anything for you, and that's what's scary. You're not the woman I fell in love with years back. I don't think she'll ever exist again. I know this meeting isn't about us, but I feel like I have to be honest with you, even if it means hurting you. I have to have his best interest in mind."

"I agree one hundred percent. It is about what's best for him, and it's always been that way. I'm so much better now."

Tommy looked at her, debating what he should do. One part of him wanted to believe her and give Tommy Jr. a chance to know his mother. He'd hate to have him grow up and find out that his father had deprived him of a relationship with his mother.

After sitting and thinking for a little while longer, Tommy decided that at this time he couldn't subject his son to a relationship with her. Not yet anyway. Not until she went to rehab as she said she would. Then she'd be proving that she had really changed. That way he could go to bed at night knowing he'd made the right decision.

Brooklyn for the first time in a long time cried because she was hurt. She thought for sure he'd look past her addiction and all of the mistakes she'd made in the past and give her a chance. She walked away from that meeting with a plan. She was going to prove herself to him and get the relationship she was looking for.

Brooklyn felt confident that she could do what she needed to do for herself and her kids. None of the things that she'd done in the past mattered if she could redeem herself by doing what was best for them in the present day and time. She truly had a chance and was going to take advantage of it.

Chapter Twenty-nine

Beginning of the End
2007

Thanksgiving Day had never been remarkable prior to this one. Turkey, baked macaroni and cheese, candied yams, collard greens and cornbread stuffing are all one could normally think of when speaking of the festivities surrounding this day of giving thanks for all of one's blessings, but on this particular day, November 25, 2007, blessings were the last thing on Brooklyn's mind. In fact, she couldn't fathom one thing to be thankful for. Not even her life felt like a blessing. Hell, for her, the energy it took just to stay alive at this point wasn't worth the misery and embarrassment.

"Hey, Brooklyn, you got a late start today, I see," one of her fellow addicts called out as she headed toward the shooting gallery upstairs.

"Yeah. Had a lot of shit on my mind, that's all. But you know me. Nothing can hold me down." She forced a laugh, though she felt like the walls were caving in on her, that she would have to fight extremely hard to pull through.

Brooklyn stood peering aimlessly out of the window as the setting sun gently displayed patches of shade onto one side of the street. A mixture of ice and snow continued to fall from the sky, turning the streets into what resembled an ice skating rink. The crackhouse, which she frequented daily to get high, was clouded with smoke, and reeked of urine and feces from the various hidden crevices where the fiends had released themselves. She felt like she wanted to puke.

She rested the right side of her thin frame up against the old wooden windowsill, her feet relaxed on the badly frayed rippled linoleum flooring. Her face full of dismay, she wasn't thinking about getting high or having jumped over the missing steps at the entrance of the building, all the while praying not to land on her ass in the basement. Nor the hole in the wall of the adjacent house that she had to climb through to get into the room where she now stood. Nor the numerous mice crawling, weaving in and out of holes in the walls, or the drug dealers in the other room selling their product to the fiends.

For the moment, all Brooklyn could think about was being just three short blocks away from her mother's home and too embarrassed to go spend the holidays with her family. She had just been diagnosed with cervical cancer and hadn't yet been able to reveal this to them. After years of unprotected sex and several untreated sexually transmitted diseases, her reckless behavior had finally run up and kicked her in the ass.

Brooklyn couldn't have cared less that she was losing her hair, or breaking out with bumps all over her face, and rashes that covered fifty percent of her body, all the result of the multiple illegal drugs she shot into her system daily. Though she'd always been the bad seed of the family, having an illness like cancer would make them feel sorry for her, and she wasn't interested in sympathy, not wanting to appear weak.

Fiends filled each room all at different levels of their high. The house was cold, only having heat in one room, which was obtained by running extension cords from the house next door. From the outside, one would assume the house was empty. With a huge orange sticker on the front of it labeling it unsafe, and the front door and most of the windows boarded up, normal people, like those not under the influence of drugs, wouldn't even be caught dead on that side of the street.

Brooklyn's mind was all over the place. She thought about her modeling career, about how'd she'd allowed herself to lose everything she'd worked for, her many failed attempts at relationships, and of course her children, one of whom she hadn't seen since he was six months old. But regardless of which path her mind would follow, the road would always end at the same destination, Dover Street.

Dover Street was in the northern part of Philadelphia. All of the houses, which were pretty small, had once been full of life and excitement but were mostly empty now. No matter how hard she tried, she could never stay away from the block very long.

This morning she woke up, quickly got dressed, and hurried to the house to try and beat the rush. Today felt different, even down to the dogs barking on the corner and the wind that blew ice in her face as she struggled to see through it. She'd arrived a few minutes later than normal and found all of her buddies already floating on cloud nine. They'd created a "snowball," a mixture of heroin and cocaine which they would place inside of a glass pipe, put fire to, and smoke. Instead of joining in, she was drawn to the window where her feet had been planted for the past twenty minutes.

Joey, one of the dealers who ran the house, yelled from the doorway, "Yo, Brooklyn, are you going to cop or what? You know you can't stay here if you're not. This ain't no goddamn recreation center!"

The vibration of Joey's voice startled everyone in the room, especially JC, who'd just wrapped his brown leather belt around his upper arm, preparing to shoot his heated concoction into his bulging vein.

Brooklyn snapped out of her daydream. She turned to face him before taking a step away from the window. "Yeah, Joey. I'm sorry. I have some shit on my mind."

Joey's look of disgust changed to anger. "Well, you know the rules," he yelled. "So what's on your mind is some personal shit that you can take outside, if you ain't getting high." He motioned his hands toward the door.

"I said I'm gonna cop, Joey. Damn! I come here every day, and I always cop, so you don't have to try to play me. Just give me a minute, OK." Brooklyn hated that her moment of deep thought had been ruined.

"Yeah, a minute is all you're gonna get too!" he roared. "I'll be back in here to check, and you better either have some money in your hand, or the handle of the front door on your way out!" He turned around and walked through the halls, checking in on some of the other patrons of the house, the thumping noises from his large feet fading as he moved away from the room.

Brooklyn wanted to get high. In fact, her body was yearning for drugs, but her troubles had a grip on her thoughts and she was having trouble releasing them as she resumed her position, staring out into the ice storm. So far, the time had gone by without incident, but it was still early. There was rarely a dull moment in the house, also known as "The Tower," where mayhem could erupt at the drop of a dime. Either someone was getting thrown out for nonpayment or being carried out when they overdosed.

She quickly turned around when she heard footsteps nearing the door. Joey was back as promised. She dug into the pocket of her jeans and pulled out the folded twenty-dollar bill she had inside. The same twenty dollars she'd earned from giving oral sex to one of the sloppiest men she'd ever seen was a few moments away from being gone with the wind. One thing about Brooklyn, she always managed to get enough money to support her habit, even if it meant stealing from her own relatives and friends.

Joey motioned with his hands for her to follow him, and she walked behind him toward the room with the drug supplies. She stopped just outside of the door, as she normally did, and waited patiently to be served like a child in the lunch line.

Joey knocked on the door, which was bolted shut, and called out the items he needed. A bodyguard stood next to Joey, his hands in his pocket, firmly gripping his handgun, in case one of the crackheads got out of hand and had to be taken care of. Through a makeshift mail slot in the center of the brown wooden door, a bag filled with vials of crack cocaine inside of a sandwich bag was passed into his hand. He turned around, took the money from Brooklyn's extended hand, and replaced it with the bag of drugs.

She then walked away, returning to the room where she was prior to walking down the long hallway with him. She grabbed a seat off to the far right side of the room and sat down, trying to get comfortable.

Brooklyn took a quick surveillance and noticed Stacey shooting a mixture that she'd just heated into her veins. Stacey's eyes rolled into the back of her head within seconds as her body relaxed and her arm rested at her side. Brooklyn stared at her, anxious to get the same feeling, but her mind was still fixated on the test results her doctor had read to her earlier in the week.

Over and over in her head, she repeated, *Cancer? How the hell did I get cancer? Out of all the ailments I could get, why cancer?*

After a few more minutes of sulking in her misery, she opened up the bag of drugs and began the steps that would land her in the relaxing state she needed to be. Ten minutes later she was in a fantasy world, still sitting in the chair, her head resting on the back of it. The room was quiet, and the smell in the air made it that much more tranquil.

She had almost fallen asleep when a loud thump stunned her. Stacey had fallen down on the floor and began convulsing. Everyone in the room was now focusing their attention on her as her body continued to jerk and foam ran out of her mouth and down the sides of her face. "Somebody call nine-one-one!" Brooklyn yelled as she got down on her knees next to her.

"Nobody move! Mack, carry her ass out and put her in the lot down the street!" Joey yelled, his tone cold and steady as ice.

Brooklyn looked at him, filled with anger. She knew from past experiences that he was heartless. Any other time she'd get into a corner and watch the drama unfold, but Stacey was one of her friends, and she wasn't ready to lose her just yet.

"Call nine-one-one now," she yelled. "Don't put her out in the street like a piece of garbage." She tried to push Mack's hands away from Stacey's body.

"Back off, Brooklyn, before I put your ass out there with her. Mack, hurry up before this bitch dies on the floor," Joey yelled back. He hated when fiends got sick in the house. He knew it was always a possibility and was seriously thinking about moving his business to another part of the neighborhood separate from where they got high.

"She'll die out there, Joey. Please don't put her out there." Brooklyn's eyes began to well up with tears. She was practically in a tug-of-war with Mack, trying to keep him from putting Stacey out.

"I don't give a fuck about that!" Joey yelled. "She's not going to die up in here and have the cops come raid my shit. Hell, naw! Mack, put that bitch out now!" He pushed Brooklyn out of the way.

Mack picked Stacey's limp body up from the floor and put her over his shoulder. Brooklyn thought for sure she was already gone. She stared back at Joey. As the two watched each other, Brooklyn briefly reminisced on the good times they'd spent together when they dated during her modeling days. The man she once cared for stared right through her, almost as if she had translucent skin. Joey gave her a look of seriousness that ended all hope she had of changing his mind. Either way, she didn't plan on leaving Stacey out there for dead alone in the storm.

Brooklyn ran out behind Mack, who was looking left and right as he hurried down the street. Tears streamed down her face as she watched the life drain out of her friend's body. Stacey looked like a rag doll as she hung over Mack's shoulder.

Mack walked into the lot and dropped Stacey down on the ground. She hit the ice-covered lot like a ton of bricks. He walked out of the lot and headed toward the house without even looking back.

Brooklyn called Mack's name as he neared the sidewalk, almost gone from her eyesight.

"What?" Mack shouted, not even turning around to face her.

"Please call nine-one-one. Please, I'm begging you," Brooklyn cried, trying to save her dying friend.

As Mack walked away, Brooklyn let out a sigh of helplessness. She took off her coat, wrapped it around Stacey's cold body, and picked her head up from the ground. Stacey's eyes were closed, and her body was quickly dropping in temperature. She was still breathing, but that didn't mean she'd make it.

Brooklyn rubbed her hand across her forehead, looking around, hoping someone would arrive to help. She kept praying that Stacey would be OK, though her mind was telling her otherwise. Her knees were becoming stiff, but she refused to move. Stacey would have done the same for her. At least she forced herself to believe that.

"Help me, please. Somebody help me!" Brooklyn screamed as she grabbed hold of Stacey's shoulders and shook her as hard as she could. "Don't die on me, Stacey, please." Stacey's lips were slowly turning blue, and as loud as Brooklyn screamed her name, she got no response. She could feel the life draining out of Stacey's body with each passing second.

How had things come to this? How had things gone so wrong? As Stacey's almost lifeless body lay in front of Brooklyn, so many thoughts ran through her mind, including the decisions that landed her where she was that day. After all, Stacey was the one who got her hooked in the first place. Was this the lesson she needed to finally quit?

Brooklyn could remember as clear as day her first hit over eighteen years ago. She could also remember the special times they'd had, regardless of how screwed up things would get. She missed her friend already, just facing the idea of losing her. She wondered what she'd do without her right hand. In her eyes, she had nothing to live for with Stacey gone. Brooklyn's family despised her, and she'd done her children so wrong, they wouldn't even speak to her, even if she entered a room in which they were seated.

Brooklyn looked down at Stacey's face and saw her own. She saw her beautiful high cheekbones, long eyelashes, almond-shaped eyes, caramel complexion, and her perfectly full lips. Actually, Brooklyn saw the way she *used* to look, instead of her thin facial structure and the red blotches that covered her sunken cheeks. She didn't see her tired eyes and the dark circles underneath them. Neither did she see her dry, cracked lips, nor her hair that was as coarse as a Brillo pad.

The beautiful woman that she used to be had disappeared. Even if she quit shooting and inhaling all of the poison she did daily, that woman could never return. So what could she do? At that moment she wished she was the one dying instead of Stacey, but then her life would most likely have been spared. Death was something she'd stared in the eye on many occasions, but for some reason, God had always left her here to see another day.

What is He trying to tell me? Is there something else that I'm supposed to be doing?

Brooklyn got up from the ground. She thought she could run and get help for Stacey if she could just pull her out of the lot and into one of the houses. She grabbed her by the arms and tried dragging her, but weighing no more than 110 pounds soaking wet, she couldn't move her more than a few inches. She got back in position beside her, deciding she'd wait there with her until someone arrived to aid them. Her own body was stiffening to the point where she could no longer feel her limbs, or even her fingers that rested on Stacey's forehead. Was she finally going to get her wish? At least that's what she hoped.

In the distance Brooklyn could hear sirens, but she couldn't move to meet them at the street. If anyone was looking for them, it would be almost impossible for the duo to be found, as the sun was going down and the alley was darkening. Her voice wasn't as loud as it was previously. In fact, she could barely catch her breath as she felt herself getting weaker by the second. Maybe this was it. Maybe this was the way her life was supposed to end—in a dark alley, like a piece of trash.

Suddenly the sirens became inaudible, and her body fell to the ground next to Stacey's. Her head rested on Stacey's arm. Her eyes slowly closed, her body mirroring the unresponsive figure next to her.

Chapter Thirty

Take Me as I Am
November 2007

Brooklyn opened her eyes and immediately noticed that she was no longer laying in the cold alley next to Stacey. As she blinked a few times to focus on her surroundings, she could hear an irritating beeping noise and the patter of feet in the hall. She tried to sit up, but something was holding her down, preventing her hands from getting loose. A chalkboard on the wall directly in front of her read "Welcome to Room 312. Get well soon!"

What the hell? she thought. By the looks of things she was in a hospital. *Why the hell are my arms tied? And where the hell is Stacey?*

Her body instantly filled with trepidation when she heard the commotion going on in the hallway just outside of the room with the nurses, doctors, and other hospital staff, and the fact that her best friend was missing in action.

She heard a voice on the intercom say, "Code eighty in Room 320, Anesthesia stat."

Brooklyn said a silent prayer hoping that it wasn't her friend who was dying in the other room. She tried again to free herself from the restraints that had her strapped to the side railings of the bed but was unsuccessful.

"Nurse! Nurse! I need a nurse in here now!" She yelled as loud as she could, but no one came. She continued to yell for the next five minutes until finally a nurse's aide entered her room.

"It's about damn time. I've been yelling for over five minutes. Why are my hands tied? And where is my friend Stacey?" she screamed, her face frowned, eyebrows raised.

"Miss, there's no need to be rude. Your hands are tied because you were combative when the ambulance was bringing you in."

"Listen, don't tell me about needs. I just woke up tied to a fucking bed and screamed for damn near ten minutes for help and no one came. So, sorry if you can't take the heat, but I need to know what the hell is going on here."

"OK, well, there is a code on the floor, so as soon as I can get a doctor to come in and talk to you, I will. In the meantime, is there anything I can get you? Maybe some water?" The nurse's aide was visibly annoyed by Brooklyn's anger. Never looking Brooklyn in the eye, she walked around to the side of the bed, picked up the pink jug filled with water, and poured some in a paper cup.

"I don't want any water. I want to know where my friend is." Brooklyn would have smacked that cup clean out of her hand if her hands were free.

"What is your friend's name?"

"Stacey Hicks," she quickly replied.

The nurse's aide looked at Brooklyn as if she had just seen a ghost. She stood there silent for a few moments before speaking. "Um, I don't recall a patient by that name, but let me check and I'll get back to you. Is there anything else before I leave?"

Feeling uneasy, Brooklyn replied, "Listen, lady, I wasn't born yesterday. Don't stand there and bullshit me. I know that if I'm here, she must've been here too, so I need to know now where the hell my friend is."

The nurse's aide looked around the room and then out toward the hallway. After a few seconds of looking back and forth, she walked toward the door and slowly closed it.

Brooklyn felt as if she was about to hear something she wasn't prepared for. As the nurse's aide was walking back over to the bed, Brooklyn started babbling. "Wait. If you're going to tell me she's dead, I don't want to know. I'm not ready to hear it. I mean, I know I asked, but I was just concerned. I know you can understand. I'm sure you have friends. I mean, she's all I have and—"

"I'm not going to tell you that she's dead, OK, so slow down. I don't have good news though, and I can get in big trouble even telling you this, but I can see how much you love her."

"Well, if she's not dead, then where is she?" She braced herself for the response. In her heart she already knew what was coming next but she also hoped that her heart was wrong.

The nurse's aide took a deep breath. "She's coding. Which means her heart stopped, and they are working hard to bring her back. All of the commotion you hear is from her room." She put her hand on Brooklyn's shoulder, to console her.

Brooklyn sat still as statue. Instantly her mind flashed back to the days when they were teenagers and all they cared about were boys, the weekend sleepovers, and the pact that they'd always be there for one another. She felt helpless because there wasn't anything she could do.

The nurse's aide felt sorry for the woman who just a few minutes earlier was ready for war. She too knew how it felt to lose someone close, her mother having passed the previous year.

"Listen, if I know anything, I know prayer helps. If it's her time to go, she'll go, but God will bring you through it."

Brooklyn still sat silent, but tears were flowing freely from her eyes. She couldn't remember the last time she'd cried. Even hearing she had cancer wasn't enough to break her down. She'd been through so much, her insides were hollow. She didn't know how to care or how to love because she didn't care about herself. If they'd told her at that very moment that she was going to die, she would've been fine with it. But she still couldn't face losing her best friend.

When the tears turned into an uncontrollable sob, the nurse's aide felt that maybe she shouldn't have been the one to relay the information. She walked over toward the cabinet near the window and retrieved a box of tissue. Then she walked back over to Brooklyn and wiped her eyes.

"Thank you," Brooklyn replied, her face filled with grief.

"I'm going to go over and check on your friend." The aide figured that was the least she could do, especially after getting her all bent out of shape. "When I find out more information, I will come back and update you."

"OK, thanks again."

Brooklyn lay staring out of the window for the next twenty minutes before a familiar voice called her name from behind the curtain. She turned to face the direction of the voice and smiled when her friend Wanda appeared.

"Wow! Look what the cat drug in." She smiled. "I would hug you, but they have my arms tied."

"Oh, hell no. We won't have that!" Wanda sat her purse down on the chair before walking over to the bed and trying to figure out how to free Brooklyn's hands from the restraints.

One hand at a time, Brooklyn was freed. She rubbed her sore wrists before sitting up and hugging the friend she hadn't seen in almost a year.

The two women rocked back and forth and laughed aloud, holding on tight to one another. After a few seconds, they let go of each other.

Wanda placed her hands on Brooklyn's shoulders and looked into her eyes. "What's been up, girl? It seems like eons since the last time I saw you."

"You know me—Same shit, running the street trying to stay alive. You look good." Brooklyn smiled. "I see life's treating you well. At least one of us is living up to the PYT name."

"You're still beautiful, Brook. Hell, I'm still jealous of you." Wanda laughed as she turned to glance out of the door. She was trying to make small talk to avoid the inevitable. Eventually she would have to give Brooklyn the bad news.

"Bullshit! You could always give me a run for my money."

"Yeah, right. Everybody wanted you, all the top hustlers, like Sincere. You were the supermodel on the runways and in the magazines. I was just the skinny chick from the projects."

"Shit. Now I'm just a crackhead with a bunch of kids spread all around North Philly, so none of that matters, right. Shit, if Sincere could see me now, he'd be disgusted."

Brooklyn was no longer laughing; in fact, her smile had turned into a frown. She began to think about Stacey again and focused on the fact since Wanda had sat down she'd kept looking out into the hallway. "So what brings you here anyway? How did you even know I was in the hospital?"

Over the years she and Wanda hadn't stayed in touch, especially during her drug binges, but she had stayed close to Stacey.

Brooklyn immediately felt a cold breeze, as if someone had just opened up a window to let Mother Nature spill into the hospital room. An inexplicable shiver took over her body as her friend stared at her with a perplexed look.

Her last round of questioning having gone unanswered, Brooklyn asked, "What's going on, Wanda?"

Wanda took a deep breath. She was afraid that her answer would devastate an already fragile woman. Carefully letting the words slip, she answered, "Brook, I have some really bad news," her voice trembling. The tears she'd been holding back began to fall freely from her eyes. "Stacey didn't make it. She died about a half-hour ago from cardiac arrest."

"No, Wanda, don't bullshit me like that."

Brooklyn got up out of the bed and ran toward the door, her body full of adrenaline. Wanda followed behind her and grabbed hold of her from behind, but Brooklyn, who'd always been the strongest of the bunch, easily pulled herself free and pushed the door open. She ran over to the nurses' station, where a couple of nurses sat talking. Her hands slammed onto the top of the counter, sending a few sheets of paper to the floor.

"Excuse me. I need to know which room is Stacey Hicks' please!" she yelled loudly. She was confused, angry, hurt, sad, and afraid all at the same time.

"How did you get your restraints loose?" The Asian nurse quickly stood up from her seat. She'd been there to witness Brooklyn kick and punch the admitting nurse when she'd arrived a few days earlier. Afraid that she too would be assaulted, she slowly moved toward the phone to call security.

"Lady, don't fuck with me! I know you speak English. Now, I said I need to know what room is Stacey Hicks'! Somebody better give me answers before I start going off!" She turned back to look at Wanda, who was standing with tears streaming down both sides of her face and falling onto her shoulders.

The Asian nurse picked up the phone and dialed security after noticing she wouldn't be able to calm the patient down.

Wanda pointed in the direction of Stacey's room without speaking.

Surprisingly, Brooklyn still hadn't shed a tear. She ran over to the room and took a deep breath before pushing the wooden door open. On the bed was a black bag that she knew contained a body, the body of her friend. She could hear Wanda in the background arguing with the guards to allow her to say her good-byes. She almost wished that they wouldn't, afraid that she'd never be able to erase the image of Stacey's dead body out of her mind.

While taking baby steps toward the bed, Brooklyn felt a hand on her shoulder. She spun around looking for a fight. It was the nurse's aide who had spoken with her earlier that day in her room.

"I'm not here to stop you. I just wanted to be here to support you."

Brooklyn didn't reply and turned back around to face the black bag. She couldn't move. Her feet felt as if they were glued to the floor. As she stood there, flashbacks of their friendship crossed her mind—Stacey would come over with her Barbie sleeping bag and they'd lie across the living room floor and watch movies. As teens they chased boys together, and as adults they got high together.

She felt someone grab her hand. She turned and saw Wanda standing next to her.

"Come on," Wanda whispered, "we'll do this together."

Wanda nodded to the nurse's aide, who had since walked over to the bed and placed her hand on the opening of the bag. Slowly she opened the bag that would reveal Stacey's face. Instantly tears poured from Brooklyn's eyes with the confirmation.

Brooklyn and Wanda walked hand and hand toward the bed. Wanda released her hold on Brooklyn's hand but stood next to her, feeling a need to support her. She'd failed as a friend and wanted to make up for all of the years they'd lost. She'd allowed envy to take hold of her emotions, and instead of taking a step closer, took two steps back. At that moment she knew she would never walk out on Brooklyn again because she couldn't bear to lose her as well.

Brooklyn was staring at Stacey and rubbing her fingers across her forehead. "I told you I wouldn't leave you. I'm right here, Stacey. I love you more than I love myself, Stacey, you hear me? Friends to the end, remember that. You were always the mushy type; now look at me crying and shit. Thought we'd never see that day." she paused. "Remember that time you broke your ankle and I laughed because you wouldn't stop crying." She laughed for a second, stopping the flow of tears.

The nurse's aide had left them alone, and Wanda stood near the door allowing Brooklyn to have one last chat before they took her away. She couldn't hold her own tears back as she dreaded the moment they'd have to pull Brooklyn away.

"Damn, Stacey, why did you have to break us up? We were supposed to get clean together. I can't do it without you. I'm not strong enough. I need you." Brooklyn cried as she put her head on the edge of the bed.

She lay there silently for the next twenty minutes without being disturbed. She knew something in her life had to change, and the day she walked out of the hospital, she planned on doing just that, making a change.

Chapter Thirty-one

Time Will Tell

"Thanks for coming, Mom. I really appreciate it!" Sasha smiled.

"I wouldn't miss this for the world. I just can't believe I'm going to be a grandmom." Brooklyn smiled as she glanced over at the monitor that showed Sasha's growing baby. Everything with the baby was perfect, not to mention, her relationship with her daughter was better than either of them could have ever expected.

Brooklyn had been clean for the past six months. Stacey's death was traumatic for her and just the thing she needed to help her kick the habit. She missed her, feeling at times like she had no one to talk to. Sure, Wanda was around, but she and Brooklyn didn't have as much in common. Their life experiences had been the total opposite of each other's, and she couldn't really relate to someone who had no clue what she'd been through. She also didn't want Wanda, or anyone for that matter, to look down on her. Most people thought of her as a survivor, but others looked at her like trash. She had learned the hard way that sometimes one's past is not easily forgotten.

After the ultrasound, the two headed home.

Sasha had recently moved in with Brooklyn and her half-sister Janelle. Janelle, the daughter of Sincere and Stacey, was as close to Brooklyn as her own mother.

After Stacey's death, Brooklyn made sure to do everything in her power to keep Janelle around.

The months passed by quickly, and Brooklyn was able to lay eyes on her granddaughter. Every pregnancy of hers had been different. Every situation that revolved around their lives was tough. Every time she gave birth, she was detached. She'd never felt the motherly connection that most women felt when they gave birth, and she saw every delivery as a problem because the fathers had been nothing but.

Sadly, for the first time in her life, she felt connected. Though the baby wasn't hers, she looked into her puffy little eyes and fell in love. When she'd learned of the cancer, she truly believed that life was over, and at that point she didn't care. With her cancer in remission and the forgiveness of her daughter, she truly believed that all of the pain was worth it. Now she had someone to live for.

There was a time when she could see herself in her daughter and prayed that somehow Sasha would ignore the temptations that she hadn't be able to resist. Now this little bundle of joy was going to make all of the difference in her life, and her relationship with Sasha was going to be stronger than ever.

Going down to Stacey's grave was a weekly ritual for Brooklyn. Oftentimes she'd be alone and would get down on her knees and chat with her friend, reminiscing on the good times they'd shared. She'd even talk about the times they argued and wanted to pull each other's hair out. Somehow, they had always been able to come back together. As many times as their friendship had been tested, they still remained friends to the end. Hell, not even Sincere could keep them apart for long.

She found that at times, when she had a lot on her mind or things she felt she couldn't share with anyone else, she'd do it there.

Brooklyn sat down next to Stacey's grave. The flowers she'd brought the previous week were withering in the extreme heat. As she sat down, she talked to her about everything that had been going on. She missed her more than anything, and you could see it every time she came to the grave site. It was almost as if her backbone was gone.

In the past Brooklyn was far from a nice person. Most people steered clear of her because they wanted to avoid a confrontation with her. She was used to fighting because running the streets for as many years as she did took courage. She was never afraid of anything or anyone, until the day Stacey died in her arms.

Looking back on all she'd been through, it was clear that every incident made her a stronger woman. She thought about the tumultuous relationship she had with her mother and her absentee father. She could even see how her failed relationships with men mirrored the many failed relationships her mother had with men. Every man Janice had been with, including her husband, walked out on her and her true love, alcohol. True, she'd slowed down but she hadn't quit.

Brooklyn, though never addicted to drinking, could relate, since drugs were at one point her kryptonite. If she could turn back the hands of time, surely she'd do a lot of things differently, but she could no longer live with regret. Life was truly worth living.

She got up from her seated position and headed out of the cemetery. She stopped short of the gates to look back. "Thanks for listening, Stacey. I love you."

ORDER FORM
URBAN BOOKS, LLC
78 E. Industry Ct
Deer Park, NY 11729

Name: (please print):_____

Address: _____

City/State: _____

Zip: _____

QTY	TITLES	PRICE

Shipping and handling-add $3.50 for 1st book, then $1.75 for each additional book.

Please send a check payable to:
 Urban Books, LLC
Please allow 4-6 weeks for delivery